Blue B

Over the jangle of gunfire, C̶l̶i̶n̶t̶ ̶h̶e̶a̶r̶d̶ ̶t̶h̶e̶ ̶s̶c̶r̶a̶p̶e̶
of iron clearing leather and a hammer clicking into place.
When he snapped his eyes toward the man wearing the
blue handkerchief over his face, Clint clearly saw the
man's pistol looking right back at him as well as the shift
of a smile forming underneath that bandanna.

When Clint heard the gunshot, his entire body twitched
in expectation of a bullet ripping through it. But the pain
didn't come and the impact of the round never arrived.

Instead, he saw Blue's head snap to one side and the
pistol fall from his hand. The bulge of his chin beneath
the bandanna dropped a little lower, and a dark crimson
stain formed in the fabric. He remained upright for a moment, but soon his entire body flopped over and the last
bit of life leaked out of him . . .

THE GUNSMITH

276

THE CANADIAN JOB

J. R. ROBERTS

JOVE BOOKS, NEW YORK

THE BERKLEY PUBLISHING GROUP
Published by the Penguin Group
Penguin Group (USA) Inc.
375 Hudson Street, New York, New York 10014, USA
Penguin Group (Canada), 10 Alcorn Avenue, Toronto, Ontario M4V 3B2, Canada
(a division of Pearson Penguin Canada Inc.)
Penguin Books Ltd., 80 Strand, London WC2R 0RL, England
Penguin Group Ireland, 25 St. Stephen's Green, Dublin 2, Ireland (a division of Penguin Books Ltd.)
Penguin Group (Australia), 250 Camberwell Road, Camberwell, Victoria 3124, Australia
(a division of Pearson Australia Group Pty. Ltd.)
Penguin Books India Pvt. Ltd., 11 Community Centre, Panchsheel Park, New Delhi—110 017, India
Penguin Group (NZ), Cnr. Airborne and Rosedale Roads, Albany, Auckland 1310, New Zealand
(a division of Pearson New Zealand Ltd.)
Penguin Books (South Africa) (Pty.) Ltd., 24 Sturdee Avenue, Rosebank, Johannesburg 2196, South
Africa

Penguin Books Ltd., Registered Offices: 80 Strand, London WC2R 0RL, England

This is a work of fiction. Names, characters, places, and incidents either are the product of the author's imagination or are used fictitiously, and any resemblance to actual persons, living or dead, business establishments, events, or locales is entirely coincidental.

THE CANADIAN JOB

A Jove Book / published by arrangement with the author

PRINTING HISTORY
Jove mass-market edition / December 2004

Copyright © 2004 by Robert J. Randisi.

ISBN: 0-515-13860-6

JOVE®
Jove books are published by The Berkley Publishing Group,
a division of Penguin Group (USA) Inc.,
375 Hudson Street, New York, New York 10014.
JOVE is a registered trademark of Penguin Group (USA) Inc.
The "J" design is a trademark belonging to Penguin Group (USA) Inc.

PRINTED IN THE UNITED STATES OF AMERICA

10 9 8 7 6 5 4 3 2 1

ONE

Winter hit the entire world without showing any preferences. When it was time for the cold to sink its teeth into the land and for the snow to fill the air, it came no matter who liked it or what got in its way. Nature was the most fair-minded lady in that respect. Of course, that also made her pretty damn harsh at times.

It had been a brutal winter, but that was no surprise to those who lived in the areas that always got hit the hardest. Folks up north were accustomed to the trials of the cold and found out real quick that complaining about it didn't do a bit of good. Some folks who lived farther south felt Nature's bite a little harder, but they kept their heads down, bundled themselves up and waited for it to pass.

And still others took a more active approach to things. They were the travelers and wanderers who moved on to better locations because they had nothing vested in struggling through a hard snap in one particular place. Clint Adams was one of the men in that category, and he made it a practice to keep moving so long as it suited him.

On some accounts, it would have been easier to settle someplace or point the nose of his Darley Arabian stallion

1

in the direction of somewhere warmer. But sometimes a man didn't feel like taking the easier trail, especially when circumstances pointed him in another direction. Clint had lived plenty of years and gotten through plenty of scrapes by being able to see where he was being led and walking in that direction rather than fighting to turn toward another. Perhaps it was not the best system, but it worked in the long run.

At least that's what he kept telling himself when things weren't going his way.

Clint had known months before it started that the winter was going to be rough. After spending more than his share of nights sleeping under the stars, he could tell the bitter cold was going to get worse. There was a steely flavor to the air that caught in the back of Clint's nose whenever he pulled in a bone-chilling breath.

The clouds rolled by overhead like dirty, shredded sheets whose only purpose was to keep the sun from warming the earth below. Snow would fall, but not before a dousing round of sleet had soaked right down to the center of Clint's body. Beneath the Darley Arabian's hooves, the ground was packed solid, every bit of moisture frozen into a hard mortar.

Despite the harsh whims of the weather, Clint found himself enjoying a good portion of it. There was a brutal simplicity to the winter that just didn't present itself during the warmer months. Summer was a whole lot of heat and insects wrapped in a sunny package that was supposed to be enjoyed just because it was so bright.

Both the heat and cold brought their share of hardship, but at least in the cold everything you needed to know was right there in front of you. When fingers and toes started to go numb, it was time to find a fire. When it got dark, it was time to find shelter. There just didn't seem to be as many gray areas in the cold, and as long as a man knew the rules, he would do just fine.

Clint was ready for some time in the cold, simply because accepting it was easier than trying to find a way out of it. Living off the land for a little while was always a good way to clear his head and let the dust settle. In Clint's life, there had been no shortage of dust-ups, and he'd learned long ago to treasure his quiet time whenever he could get it.

Not only that, but after tending to some business in northern California and Oregon, Clint found himself deep enough within the snow-covered part of the country that riding out would have been too much trouble. A big part of survival was knowing the lay of the land. The simple truth of the matter was that there was more to the Northeast than there was to the South. And with the winter baring its teeth the way it was, Clint was in no mood to backtrack.

It was the end of January and the trees on cither side of Clint's path resembled skeletal fingers reaching up through the dirt. The wind howled through them and caused each bare branch to wave back and forth as he rode by.

Clint's stallion, Eclipse, was handling the weather well enough. The Darley Arabian was in constant motion so his muscles warmed nearly every inch of his body. The animal's breath came out from his nostrils in gouts of steam as his powerful neck churned his head back and forth.

Clint's gloved hands were wrapped tightly around the reins, guiding Eclipse toward the sparse outlines on the horizon. One of the other reasons for Clint to venture into the Oregon territory was to meet up with a fellow he owed a favor to from several years back. The man's name was Bobby Hill and the last time Clint had seen him, Bobby had been making his living bringing in men wanted by the U.S. government.

One of the things about spending time in California

was that it was a little harder to keep out of sight. That became even harder when a man's name was as well known as Clint Adams's. The last time Clint had been in San Francisco, his name had been tossed about a little more than usual, which was how Bobby found out that Clint was there.

Before Clint could get too far away from civilization, a message from Bobby found its way to him and gave Clint a nudge in the direction he eventually decided to ride. The message hadn't said much, but then again Bobby was never much of a talker. It hadn't even been too insistent—more of a friendly request than anything else.

Clint figured the world turned a lot smoother when men helped each other out and lived up to their debts. So rather than ignore the message that Bobby had gone through the trouble to send and fight the other signals pushing him in a certain direction, Clint had pointed Eclipse north and snapped the reins.

That had been a week ago.

In that time, Clint had had plenty of time to rethink his decision, but it was too late to turn back now. He hoped it was just the cold in his bones that made him wonder if he'd ridden in the right direction.

TWO

The message had instructed Clint to meet Bobby in a place called Krieger's Pass. There had been some sketchy directions to keep Clint from getting lost, but once he'd arrived, Clint was surprised he'd found the place at all. He wasn't certain about how many people had to live in a place for it to be considered a town, but Krieger's Pass seemed barely big enough to count as a settlement.

What few structures there were appeared ready to collapse: they were being held up by several thick pieces of lumber nailed here and there as supports. If not for the ground being frozen hard as brick beneath a loose layer of dust, those supports would have surely slid out of place to let the buildings fall like dominoes.

Clint rode in on one of two or three paths that could just pass as streets. Besides being crooked as hell, they were only wide enough here and there for two horses to walk side by side. By the time he got into the middle of town, Clint saw that there were actually only two streets, but they intersected at such awkward angles that it gave the impression there were more. The population of the settlement struck him in much the same way. Although only a few people were wandering here and there, the close quarters caused by the leaning buildings made it seem as if there were twice as many.

Having come in from the open trail, Clint couldn't help feeling anxious as he rode further into Krieger's Pass. The sounds of people living in close proximity rattled along the rickety walls. Nobody could walk anywhere near him without almost bouncing straight into him.

Before long, Clint's mind adjusted to being in town as opposed to riding in the open. His eyes quickly picked out the places he needed such as a bed for the night and some food for his belly. No sooner had he decided on a place to eat than he was stopped by a slight figure wearing dirty clothes.

"Hold on for a second, mister," the person said.

Clint didn't have a clear view of the person because Eclipse's head obscured the stranger's face. Pulling back on the reins, Clint shifted in his saddle to get a better look. "It doesn't seem like I have much choice," he said to whoever was in front of him.

Suddenly, the other person stepped around Eclipse so as to get a clear look up at Clint. Less than a second later, another horse and rider came walking along heading straight for the figure.

Clint didn't have much of a chance to see the other person before he reached down and took hold of the stranger's arm. Lifting up while steering Eclipse toward the side of the street, he swung the person out of the way of the oncoming rider.

The first thing Clint noticed was how light the person was. The next thing was the strands of blond hair that dropped down from beneath the person's hat and over a surprised face. Swinging down from the saddle, Clint landed on a few planks lying next to each other—the town's excuse for a boardwalk.

"You all right?" he asked.

While the other person's face might have been dirty

and flushed, there was no mistaking the femininity of her features. The eyes that darted back and forth between Clint and the backside of the horse that had almost run her over were wide and an earthy shade of brown.

"Even after being here for nearly a month," she said, "I'm still not used to these damn streets. I feel like this whole town's about to drop in on top of my head at any minute."

"Glad to know I'm not the only one. Now, you mind telling me why you stopped me like that?"

Batting her eyes a few times in a flustered way, she asked, "You're Clint Adams, aren't you?"

Clint paused before answering the question, just to see if she would start to squirm. It took only a few seconds, but she started squirming sure enough. Finally letting her off the hook, he said, "Yeah. I'm Clint Adams."

She let out a breath. "Oh good. For a moment I thought I risked my neck to talk to the wrong man."

As he stood in front of the blonde, Clint realized that heading his way was yet another set of hooves, this time pulling a one-seat buggy down the crooked street. He pressed up against his stallion as the buggy scraped by behind him, but it was not a position he was comfortable with.

"Is there anywhere we can go that's not in the middle of all this commotion?" Clint asked.

The blonde shrugged and replied, "I know someplace we can get off this street."

"Is there something to eat and drink there as well?"

"Yep."

"Even better. Lead the way."

Turning in a tight half-circle that showed she was a little more accustomed to the cramped confines, the blonde faced the other side of the street, took a breath and dashed across. Although she was nearly knocked off her feet once or twice, she made it without getting more than a few jostling close calls.

Clint snapped Eclipse's reins around the closest hitching post he could find and made sure that the stallion wouldn't get trampled himself. As a few other horses were tied to the same post and were doing all right, Clint figured the Darley Arabian would be safe enough for a while.

Keeping his eyes on the blonde while scrambling across the street, Clint saw that she was leading him to a row of narrow storefronts that looked about ready to fall over. Given his own constant motion and the haphazard positioning of the signs, Clint could only guess that she was taking him to Bob's Place.

Wherever she was going, he just hoped he'd make it there in one piece.

THREE

Under normal circumstances, Clint would have found the little restaurant to be too crowded for his liking. But compared to the chaos on the street outside, Bob's Place seemed just fine. The blonde was already inside and headed toward a table near the window. She didn't take her eyes off the table until she was lowering herself into one of the chairs around it. When she looked up at him, her eyes sparkled with genuine victory.

Clint pushed past several others who'd been heading for the same table and quickly realized why she seemed so happy with her choice of seats. Not only was the table the last available one in the room, but it was also being circled by several others who seemed ready to pick her up and move her somewhere else.

The hungry looks on those faces melted away once they saw Clint walk up to the table and take a seat. After that, Clint felt like he'd won a victory as well.

At the same time they both let out a breath, which quickly turned into a round of comfortable laughter. Looking back on the last minute or two, Clint couldn't help but feel as if he'd trudged his way across a battlefield instead of crossed a street. Going by the look on her face, the blonde was feeling the same way.

"My name's LeAnne."

"That's a pretty name."

"It's actually Leigh Anne, but rather than go by one or the other, I just stuck them both together."

"Pleased to meet you, LeAnne. I guess my next question is how you spotted me through all these people."

"That one's easy," came a voice that boomed over all the other conversations being held in the room. "I told her to look for the ugliest cuss sitting on top of the prettiest horse."

As Clint rose and turned to face the approaching figure, a big smile spread across his face. "I swear I'd knock your teeth out if I didn't know it would only make you look better than you do now," Clint said. Despite his sentiment, his smile remained.

The other man's smile got bigger. Bobby Hill was a short, squat man with a head covered in blond stubble. The stubble on his face was only slightly longer and a bit darker than the stubble on his scalp, giving him the appearance of a stout rock covered in moss.

Bobby's facial features were expressive and his eyes were alight with a lively fire. Stepping up to Clint, he slapped away the hand he was being offered and wrapped both arms around him in a powerful bear hug instead. Almost lifting Clint off the ground, he said, "I wasn't sure you'd get here, but hot damn! Am I glad to see you."

"All right, all right," Clint said. "Don't get yourself worked up too much. You didn't say anything about this in your message."

Letting Clint go, Bobby walked around the table in short, waddling steps. "Yeah, well you can't fault me for being happy to see an old friend. How've you been doing?"

"I can't complain."

Bobby turned to LeAnne and said, "Listen to him, will ya? This one here's been living the high life in San Francisco and all he says is he can't complain. I heard you even got yourself part of a saloon not too far from there, Clint."

"Word travels fast," Clint replied. What he didn't mention was that it quite often traveled much faster than he would have liked.

"It certainly does, my friend. It certainly does."

Just then, a young woman wearing a plain brown dress approached the table and set down three cups of piping hot coffee. Getting a look at Clint, she smiled and lingered in front of him, bending over to give him a nice view of her smooth, pert breasts.

"That's fine, Stacy," Bobby said. "Go on and bring the rest over here before Clint starves to death."

Clint noticed the way Bobby looked at Stacy. She couldn't have been too far into her twenties and was a fine-looking woman, but Bobby watched her with a different kind of interest than the kind she had shown for Clint. As she walked away, Bobby continued watching her while shaking his head.

"She's been with me since she wasn't tall enough to look over this table," Bobby said. Jabbing a finger toward Clint, he added, "And Gunsmith or not, I'll have words with you if I think you're getting too close to that girl."

His suspicions more than confirmed, Clint lifted both hands and said, "Point taken. Can I have a sip of this coffee or is that off limits too?"

Fixing his glare on him for another second, Bobby finally lowered his hand and nodded. "That'll be fine. I hope you're hungry though."

Before Clint could ask why he'd said that, Stacy returned with her hands full of plates heaping with food. Another plate balanced on her forearm, and she expertly set them onto the table before straightening up and letting her eyes settle on Clint once more.

"Anything else I can get for you?" Stacy asked. To Clint specifically, she added, "Anything at all?"

Bobby was the one to answer that question and he did so in a tone that made her take instant notice. "No, Stacy. There's plenty of other customers in here to keep you busy."

Grudgingly, Stacy moved away from the table and was quickly absorbed into the teeming masses waiting to be served. Clint was amazed at how quickly she was swallowed up. Then again, thinking back to how the street had almost eaten him alive, that wasn't such a surprising sight after all.

"How long have you been here, Bobby?" Clint asked.

"Oh, a few years or so. This town's not so bad once you get used to it. A bit crowded, to be sure, but that's just because it's booming. I bought this restaurant a while ago and let someone else run it until I decided to retire. Well, after nearly getting my head blown off a while back, that retirement plan looked even better."

"What happened?"

Shaking his head, Bobby dismissed the question with a wave.

LeAnne seemed only too happy to take up the slack. "We went after Karl Mason down in Dodge City. Turns out that Bobby here forgot we were supposed to be after the Mason *brothers*."

"Simple mistake," Bobby clarified. "Could'a happened to anyone."

"That simple mistake crept up behind Bobby when he had one of the brothers tied up and damn near sent him to—"

"I think Clint gets the point, LeAnne." Bobby shifted uncomfortably in his seat. "No need to beat a dead horse."

"It would've been more than just a dead horse if I

hadn't been there to cover your back," LeAnne pointed out. Turning to Clint, she said, "I got to my gun quick enough to put one of the brothers down. We didn't find out that there was a third until we cashed in at the Marshal's office."

"I guess that one skinned out of there before he got what was coming to him." Glancing over to LeAnne, Bobby saw the way she rolled her eyes. He turned back to Clint and added with a shrug, "What can I say? I know how to pick my partners."

"So you're retired from chasing down bounties," Clint said. "And none too soon by the sound of it. Why send the message?"

Bobby set both hands flat upon the table and leaned forward with an unmistakable gleam in his eyes. "Because, my friend, there are some jobs that are just too good to pass up."

FOUR

Clint recognized the spark in Bobby's eyes all right. It was something all too familiar to a man who spent time sitting around a card table.

It was greed and Bobby reeked of it.

"I'm not what you might call a religious man," Clint said. "But sometimes there just isn't a way to mistake the signs the world tends to show you. Sounds to me like you were right in retiring after what happened in Dodge."

"Aw, it was a mistake, Clint. I'm not perfect."

"For a bounty hunter, that was a damn stupid mistake and you know it. You're lucky to be alive."

Bobby lowered his head and nodded. Holding out his hands and leaning back in his seat he said, "When you're right, you're right. It was time to retire and that's just what I did."

"Is it? So what was this big opportunity you were talking about in that message?"

Bobby shifted his eyes upward and put on a knowing smirk. "That piqued your interest, did it?"

"I'm here, aren't I?"

"Yes you are, so why don't we have our meals and talk about that message I sent to you?"

Up until now, Clint hadn't really paid too much attention to the food that had been served to him. He was plenty hungry, but there had been too much going on for him to notice the emptiness in his stomach. When he looked down at the plate, he spotted a thick cut of beef and huge baked potato split open and filled with butter.

"You look hungry enough to take a bite out of that plate, Clint. Eat up and I'll talk."

Clint had no problem with that plan and started cutting into his steak. The knife slid through the tender meat, which was soon melting in his mouth. It was so good, in fact, that he had to fight to keep some of his focus on what Bobby was saying.

"It's an easy enough job," the squat man said. "A man needs to be transported to this little town just this side of the Canadian border. I'd do it myself, but my days in that line of work seem to have run their course."

"I'll say," LeAnne chimed in.

"He's been cooling his heels in the jail here in town since he was brought in a week ago."

"A week?" Clint asked.

"Thereabouts," Booby replied. "I didn't plan on holding him much longer than that, but I figured I'd give you plenty of time to get here."

"Who is this fellow?"

"Just another asshole with a price on his head."

"And how is it that he got sent your way?"

"I played a part in tracking him down and bringing him in." Suddenly, the table rattled and Bobby jumped in his seat. A painful look came onto his face as he reached down to rub his shin. "All right, all right," he said to the blonde who'd just kicked him. "LeAnne brought him in, but I was the one to track him down. I may be retired, but I sure as hell ain't useless."

LeAnne shrugged and conceded that point, albeit grudgingly.

"Sounds like she's capable enough," Clint said with a mouth half full of baked potato. "Why not just have LeAnne take him north?"

"Because this man doesn't exactly ride alone," Bobby answered. "The rest of his gang aren't known men, but they're a mean bunch. At least, the prices on their heads weren't enough to justify the risk of rounding them all up. The asking price for our man to be brought in is more than enough to make it worth the effort, though."

LeAnne looked over at Clint while holding her fork halfway between her plate and mouth. "He's got to be brought in alive for it to be worth all of this. That's where things get sticky."

"Which is exactly why I thought you'd be the perfect man for this job," Bobby said. "After the times we've had together, I know you're the sort of man who keeps other men alive rather than gunning them down. But if push comes to shove, you're not the kind to back down, either."

"And?" Clint asked, knowing full well that there had to be more to it than that.

Bobby took up his knife and fork in both hands so he could start sawing away at his steak. Even after he'd cut through the tender meat, his nervous motions kept right on going. Finally, he stuck some food into his mouth and said, "And I know I couldn't do this myself. You know. After what happened in Dodge, let's just say . . ." He trailed off, swallowed his food and rolled his eyes. "Aw hell, Clint, don't make me say it."

Bobby was no longer the bounty hunter he used to be. That much was obvious. He'd either lost his edge over the years or wasn't as quick on the draw. He could have just developed a healthy case of fear after seeing the comforts of a settled life up close and personal. Whichever it was, Bobby was obviously embarrassed to admit to it.

Since he could see more than enough on the other man's face, Clint wasn't about to put Bobby against a wall. "So this is just a transport job, huh?" Clint asked.

Bobby leaned forward once again, his mind switching back onto the proper track. "Not just a transport job. It's *the* transport job. It's the kind of job that a man in my line of work dreams about, and it pays enough so that everyone getting any part of it will walk away the better for it."

"What's the catch?"

"Well, you came all this way, so I won't lie to you. It pays so much because it'll be a hard ride at the worst time of year to make it. You'll be going up north to deliver this fella to the Canadian authorities, and even though they want this man badly, they're not willing to make the ride themselves to come get him. They are willing to pay out the snoot to have him brought to them, however."

Clint mulled that over as he chewed a few more bites of steak. "Why the Canadians?" he asked. "And why won't the U.S. Marshals just take him there?"

Shrugging, Bobby started picking at his own food. Before he could say anything, LeAnne stepped in.

"If the Marshals take him, we won't get our full share. I've had enough experience to know that for damn sure. Besides, the Federals don't come up here too often, and the sooner we get this man delivered and out of our sight, the better."

"What about that gang you mentioned?" Clint asked.

Bobby swallowed what he'd been chewing and said, "They'll be after you to free him. They've dogged our trail a few times getting him here and if you ask me, I'd say they're willing to kill whoever it takes to set him loose. Of course, if you listen to the man himself . . ."

"What?" Clint asked once Bobby trailed off. "What does he say?"

"I've made it a habit not to listen to them that I track down on account of they'll say anything to get you to drop your guard or let them go. They promise money and all sorts of things, but it's just to give them a chance at freedom.

"This one's been saying a whole lot and I wonder if there's more that he's not telling." Bobby tossed aside the thought with another shrug. "Whatever it is, the Canadians are paying plenty and I know they're good for it."

"Well I still think there's more to it," LeAnne said. "I found that there's usually some grain of truth hidden in all the bullshit that outlaws say. Most of 'em are good liars, but sometimes you just know when there's something else there. I can't really explain it. You just . . ."

"You just know," Clint said, picking up the strand when LeAnne trailed off. "I understand that perfectly."

Just then, Clint and the blonde met each other's gaze, and all the chaos around them seemed to fade. At that moment, something passed between them that said more than any other words could say.

"This job can make us all rich," Bobby said. Lowering his voice, he added, "Besides that, it just needs to get done."

"Now we're getting to it," Clint said. "Tell me the rest."

"There's not much else to say. It's just that . . . well . . . it's them others that've been coming after him. They've been coming pretty steady and they know where I'm keeping him. They also know that I'm the one keeping him."

"And you're worried about them coming after you?"

"Not so much worried," Bobby said. "It's more like I'm certain. They've tried a few times, but luck and old habits have kept me in this world. I just don't know how long those two will hold out."

"All right then. Looks like I need to talk to this fellow you've got locked up."

"So you'll take the job?"

"Well," Clint said, "I sure didn't come all this way for nothing."

FIVE

After they were done eating, Clint asked if LeAnne could show him to where the captured man was being held. Bobby gave Clint a knowing wink and agreed to the request, thinking he knew exactly that Clint's intentions were. Rather than explain himself, Clint played along and returned the smirk before walking out behind LeAnne.

Once outside, Clint and LeAnne reacquainted themselves with the hectic motion flowing up and down the street like blood through excited veins. It was amazing how so few people could seem like so many. Clint even took a moment to count the heads he could see and realized that there weren't many more around than there'd be in any fair-sized town. It was just the layout of the place that clogged everything up.

Thankfully, LeAnne led him along the side of the street without making an attempt to cross. Even so, the people knocked them both around as they tried to make their way over the crooked boardwalk without tripping over the randomly placed boards. LeAnne had been in Krieger's Pass longer, so her steps were a bit more sure than Clint's. For his part, he was glad to keep himself from falling on his face.

Turning a corner, Clint found himself in somewhat less frantic surroundings. There weren't as many storefronts, which also meant there weren't nearly as many people vying for the limited space.

"It's just down here," LeAnne said, pointing to a row of buildings that looked a little sturdier than the rest. "The law around here has their hands full, so they don't do much other than put our man up in a cell."

"I'll bet."

"Even that much will change the moment that cell's needed for a local matter. Jim Masters—that's the peace-keeper around here—already told Bobby that he's one hair away from charging rent to keep that cell occupied. Once that happens, our man'll be turned out, no ifs, ands or buts."

Taking a few quick steps, Clint caught up to her enough to step in front of her. Only then did LeAnne come to a stop, and when she looked up at him, the surprise on her face quickly faded.

"I wanted to get you away from Bobby for a moment because I wanted to ask you something," Clint said.

She lowered her eyes and then glanced up at him again. This time, her expression was much warmer and a sly smile crept across her lips. "I kinda figured. What's on your mind?"

"Bobby's scared, isn't he?"

Clint could tell by the startled look on her face that that wasn't the question she'd expected him to ask. She seemed hesitant to say anything until she got over the initial shock of the question, but that was enough to tell Clint a hell of a lot.

"He's got good reason to be scared," she said before too long. "What he said about being caught flat-footed in Dodge was no lie. He nearly died that day. I was there. I thought I was going to see his head get blown clean off his shoulders. Since then, he hasn't been the same."

"Nobody can blame him for that."

"Of course not, and I don't either. But this job came along, and even I told him it sounded like a good one to retire on. But once this trouble started, it made me think twice." She paused for a moment and stepped to one side so she could lean against the closest building.

"I don't know how much tracking you've done, Clint, but I've done a fair amount and it just follows that you stop asking too much about the men you go after. They all have their stories, but they're all just telling them so they can get something over on you. If you listen, you'll either get hurt or lose your man altogether.

"But after seeing what's been going on, I can't help thinking that there's more heat around this job than we thought. The only problem is that we're in too deep to get out of it now. Even if we let him go, I think the others that are after him will keep coming to take me and Bobby down just to tie up the loose ends."

"And what about this man you tracked down?" Clint asked. "What can you tell me about him?"

"What do you want to know?"

"First of all, I want to know how you found him. Was it easy? Was he hiding very well? Did he put up much of a fight?"

"After hearing how dangerous he was, I took my time and let him wear himself out running before I got too close. By the time I closed in on him, he'd been riding for two weeks straight and getting hardly any sleep at all. He tried to get away, but when he saw he'd been found, he was too damn tired to do much about it."

Nodding, Clint said, "Good strategy."

"As for the rest of it, I can run down the list of warrants out for him if you'd like. It's really not too impressive, but what it all boils down to is that he's a dangerous man with more dangerous men working for him.

"The Canadians are willing to pay to get him back, but

the price drops to the ground if he's dead. They get kind of sketchy about what exactly he did up there, but whatever it was, they want to be the ones to punish him for it. That's for damn sure."

"Sounds like you know your business pretty well."

"Bobby taught me plenty of things," LeAnne replied.

"Were they all about tracking bounties?"

Smiling a bit, she stepped up and slid one hand along the back of Clint's neck so she could pull him closer to her face. From there, she stretched up to place a quick kiss on his upper lip. That one was followed by another, which lingered for a bit longer on his bottom lip. Her hand pulled him in even closer, then she tilted her head slightly and pressed her mouth firmly against his.

The kiss lasted just long enough for Clint to start to feel it in his toes. Just as he reached out for her, LeAnne pulled back and slipped her hand off of Clint's neck so it could trail over his chest before she dropped it to her side.

"He only taught me about bounty hunting," she said. "I learned plenty of other things on my own."

Watching her turn and head for the jailhouse, Clint said, "I'll just bet you did."

SIX

His name was Russ O'Connover. Since both Bobby and LeAnne were professional man hunters, they rarely referred to their targets in anything but the simplest of terms. To them, O'Connover was just another job, much as each head of cattle was to a rancher or cowboy: just another part of the herd and nothing more.

That was something that set bounty hunters apart from most others. They were cold when they needed to be, which was a lot of the time. They had to distance themselves from the person they were after because they might eventually be called on to put a bullet through that same person's head. Too much emotion on the job could mean that the hunter would be the one taking the bullet.

Clint understood that line of thinking. He didn't necessarily agree with it, but he understood it. There was plenty of money to be made collecting bounties but very few hunters who could make it a career. It was a job tainted by a lot of blood. From what he'd seen so far, however, Clint was certain that this job was at least being done right.

The jailhouse wasn't much more than a sturdy shack split into three little rooms. Those rooms weren't much bigger than closets and were sectioned off by rusty iron bars that had obviously been salvaged from some other source.

The air reeked of human waste and rusted water. Cold from the outside filled the place the instant LeAnne pushed the door open so she and Clint could step inside. By the looks of it, those old bars and the frozen ground were the only things keeping the jailhouse from falling in on itself. In a strange way, Clint figured, it was a good system: if the prisoners rattled the bars too much or stirred up too much fuss, the house would just cave in on top of them.

"The law knows me and Bobby, so they let us come and go as we please," LeAnne said. "Besides, we're the only ones who lock up any dangerous sorts. The rest are just drunks or rowdies from the saloon."

Though two of the three cells were occupied, Clint didn't have to ask which one held O'Connover. One of the prisoners sat propped against his bars, snoring loudly. Because of the tight quarters, the prisoner's legs stuck out from between the bars. His boots twitched every so often like a dog that was dreaming of chasing rabbits.

The other captive had been watching the front door from the moment Clint and LeAnne had arrived. Judging by the steely desperation in his eyes, the man probably hadn't looked away from that door since he'd been locked up.

"Who's this?" O'Connover asked through the thick tangle of dark red whiskers sprouting from his chin and upper lip.

"This," LeAnne replied, "is Clint Adams. He'll be coming along for the ride when we take you up to Canada."

O'Connover had been half leaning, half squatting against the wall. Pushing up with both legs, he stood and approached the bars, being careful not to get too close.

Clint saw plenty in the other man's eyes. There was a certain wildness that came from being caged like an animal, but there was also an edge that could never be learned. It was an edge that a man either had or he didn't; Russ O'Connover had it in spades.

"Clint Adams, huh?" O'Connover said. "Is he supposed to scare me?"

LeAnne stepped right in front of the cell as if to remind its inhabitant that she'd been one of the main people to put him there. "No. I just thought you should know that we're moving out soon and if you had any big ideas about getting away, you should know who you'll be going up against."

O'Connover let out a breath while shifting his eyes to look over LeAnne's shoulder to where Clint was standing. "Might as well put that pistol of yours to my head now, Gunsmith. It'd save you all a hard ride through the snow."

Clint put his hand on LeAnne's shoulder as a gentle request for her to step aside. She responded by taking two steps to the left but kept herself pointed in O'Connover's direction.

"What brings you here, Russ?" Clint asked.

Nodding toward LeAnne, he replied, "She did. Along with a few of her friends."

"They didn't come after you for no good reason, did they?"

After a moment, O'Connover shook his head and took his eyes away from LeAnne. "No. She didn't."

"So what are you wanted for? Most men with such a hefty price on their heads are more than willing to list off their accomplishments. I mean, it's not like it makes much difference now anyway, right?"

"Guess not. But what the hell are you so curious about?"

Clint didn't answer. Instead, he kept his eyes steady and fixed on O'Connover. There was no threat in his stare or even much emotion. His face became a slab of rock that gave no hints as to what was going on underneath.

Finally, O'Connover couldn't stare at the rock slab any longer. "You want me to stand here and confess to you? If that's the way it is, then you can go to hell, because I'll be making my peace with the Lord above soon enough.

"You want to hear that I killed men? Yeah, I killed plenty. You want to hear that I stole? Fine, I stole. If you're really Clint Adams, then I may just have some more to tell you that you ain't gonna like."

"Really? What's that?"

O'Connover shook his head. "For all I know, you could be some gunman spouting off at the mouth."

"So how do you want me to—"

But Clint's question was cut short by the sound of something slamming against the jailhouse. The impact shook just about every wall of the little building. Clint spun around to face the direction of the commotion, which was in the vicinity of the front door. His hand dropped toward the modified Colt at his side, but he didn't plan to draw until he had a definite target in sight.

In his cell, O'Connover was smirking. "Looks like you'll get your chance to prove yourself right about now."

SEVEN

Clint could hear the sound of labored breathing coming from the other side of the jailhouse door. That half second of listening told him everything he needed to know.

"Stop," Clint said in a quick, insistent whisper.

LeAnne had been walking toward the door with gun already drawn. She'd reached out for the handle and was just about to pull it open when Clint's voice stopped her cold. She turned around to look at him for an explanation, but all she got was a firm grip around her arm and then a strong pull that took her away from the door altogether.

Just as she cleared the spot, the door was knocked in so powerfully that it was almost taken off its hinges. Clint plucked the Colt from its holster out of pure reflex, but he kept from pulling the trigger. Someone rushed in through the doorway, but in a stumbling motion rather than a charge.

That man's face was bloodied and his expression was fear incarnate. All the color drained from his skin when he saw the two pistols pointed in his direction.

"Don't shoot!" the chubby man in the doorway said.

LeAnne managed to fight back her impulse to fire, but she couldn't quite figure out what had happened. Clint, on the other hand, was already reacting to the situation.

The man in the doorway struggled to talk, but his words were sucked even further back into his throat when he saw Clint come rushing at him. "No, no! Please, I—"

Clint put his free hand on the man's shoulder and shoved him down so hard that there was no way for him to resist. The man dropped down and stayed there, placing both arms over his head as Clint stepped completely over his huddled form.

Realizing that the man on the ground had been slammed against that door and pushed inside as a distraction, Clint was determined to keep himself ready for anything. Of course, that was easier said than done given all the angles he'd have to watch once he left the confines of the jailhouse.

Clint's eyes took in as much as they could in as little time as possible. Since that other fellow had been slammed into the closed door, Clint knew the one who'd done the shoving couldn't be far away. He spotted a few people standing nearby but none that seemed overly suspicious. Before he took his second step outside, Clint glanced to his right and found nothing but cold air. He shifted his glance to the left and managed to catch sight of a dark blur of motion. He felt the first jolt of pure adrenalin rush through his system.

Compared to the reflexive rush he'd gotten when the door had been knocked open, this second taste set his blood on fire. That was how it felt to be tossed into the mix, and that feeling was the very thing that kept a man alive.

Before he even knew what was coming at him, Clint reacted to the sight of movement. He crouched down low and took half a step back, allowing whatever it was to sail over his head followed by a deep rush of air.

If the wooden plank had made contact, it would have knocked Clint into the following week. As it was, the thick piece of wood cracked against the side of the jail-house hard enough to splinter both the plank as well as the wall.

In the blink of an eye, Clint got his bearings and sur-veyed his position. In front of him stood a man who still had both hands wrapped around the plank intended to cave in Clint's skull. The man was armed with a gun as well, but that was all Clint took the time to observe.

Already crouched down low in front of the other man, Clint reached out with his free hand and grabbed hold of the man's ankle. Clint pulled, bringing the man tumbling to the ground. It wasn't a graceful journey, to be certain. As he fell, the man tried to regain his balance or latch onto something to stop his descent. The result was a whole lot of flailing and flapping before he landed in an awkward heap.

The board the man had been holding knocked against the wall several times and even clipped Clint's shoulder, but there wasn't nearly enough force behind it to do any damage. By the time the man's back hit the ground, Clint was upright and bringing his foot down in a short, pow-erful stomp.

Clint's boot heel made contact with its target, slam-ming against the plank and pinning it to the ground. From this new vantage point, Clint was able to get a look at the man's face and quickly saw that it was covered by a dark blue bandanna.

"What the hell are you waiting for?" Blue Bandanna asked.

The only part of the man's face not covered by the bandanna was his eyes, so they were the only features Clint could see. Those were all he needed, however. Fol-lowing their gaze, Clint realized that Blue's question wasn't meant for him. Instead, those eyes were pointed away from the jailhouse.

Clint took a glance in that direction himself and saw

across the narrow street a figure standing with his head down. As soon as that figure lifted his chin to reveal a face covered by a dirty red bandanna, Clint needed only one guess as to what would happen next. Even as Red Bandanna was tossing his coat open so he could bring out the rifle hidden within, Clint was pushing himself off the ground with both feet.

Clint reached out with both hands as he launched himself into the air. It was a quick lunge and he didn't know exactly where he would land. The only thing on Clint's mind was to get the hell out of that spot.

Though no more than a second had ticked by, Clint felt as if he was moving too damn slowly. The rifle barked once, spitting out a cone of smoke and sparks as a piece of hot lead whipped through the air.

Clint's fingertips scraped along the ground first, driving into the dirt with all of his body's weight behind them. Twisting himself around, he hoped to land on his side so he could answer the rifle's thunder without knocking all of the wind from his lungs in the process. His left shoulder bumped against the earth next, which put him in a good enough position to squeeze off one round.

The Colt bucked against his palm a split second after the rifle's round took a healthy bite from the door frame. Red showed his grit when he only ducked slightly at the sound of the Colt, keeping his rifle pointed in Clint's direction.

Meanwhile, Blue was already sliding away from the door while struggling to get both legs beneath him. His hand was slapping against his side, making hasty grabs for the pistol strapped there.

Red pulled his trigger again, but his shot buried itself into the wall well above Clint's head. His aim was affected by the incoming fire from the Colt, but not as much as Clint expected. Red's eyes still fixed on his target, and he corrected his aim as he levered in a fresh round.

Once the rest of his body dropped onto the ground, Clint was steady enough to extend his right arm and aim the Colt as if he were simply pointing out his target to the Grim Reaper. He pulled his trigger once and then once again just to be sure. Clint's first shot caught Red in the midsection and the second plowed through his heart.

Even over the jangle of gunfire in his ears, Clint suddenly heard the distinctive sound of iron clearing leather and a hammer clicking back into place. When he snapped his eyes toward where Blue was lying, Clint saw the man's pistol looking right back at him as well as the shift of a smile forming beneath the blue bandanna.

EIGHT

When Clint heard the gunshot, his entire body twitched in expectation of a bullet ripping through it. His chest pinched and his gut seized into a tight knot. But the pain didn't come and the impact of the round never arrived.

Instead, he saw Blue's head snap to one side and the pistol fall from his hand. The bulge of his chin beneath the bandanna dropped a little lower, and a dark crimson stain formed in the fabric. The man remained upright for a moment, but soon his entire body flopped over and the last bit of life leaked out of him.

Clint got himself up the moment he realized he hadn't been shot. With the Colt clenched tightly in hand, he looked around for another threat, but he saw only LeAnne standing just inside the jailhouse. Her hands were still pointing the gun at Blue, and smoke was still drifting up from the barrel.

He looked into her eyes and gave her a reassuring smile. Although a little rattled, she was holding up pretty well and returned his smile with a shaky one of her own.

"Keep an eye on him," Clint said, nodding quickly toward O'Connover. "I'll see if there's any more masked men lurking about."

LeAnne steadied herself with a deep breath and moved her pistol away from the dead man lying just outside the door.

Keeping his Colt at hip level, Clint searched the street for any other threatening figures. Anyone who'd been nearby had cleared out as soon as the shooting had started. That left only a handful of people poking their noses around corners and a few huddling against a wall, frozen in their tracks.

Clint made it to where Red was lying without spotting any other masked faces. He knew that didn't guarantee there were no others around, but he also knew there wasn't enough time to scour the entire town. Picking up the rifle lying near Red's body, Clint walked around the jailhouse and scouted as much as he could before heading back to where LeAnne was waiting for him.

Once inside, Clint shut the jailhouse door and propped the rifle against the wall farthest from the occupied cells. "Something tells me that's not the first time that's happened," he said after catching his breath.

LeAnne holstered her pistol and took hold of the rifle. "They're getting bolder, that's for sure. And this is the first time we managed to get a shot off."

Clint looked out at the bodies lying on the cold ground. "We managed a bit more than that, I'd say."

Following Clint's line of sight, LeAnne took a lingering look at the bodies and felt the air become that much colder. "They told Bobby they'd be coming," she said quietly. "That's when he knew he'd be needing extra help. He didn't want it to come to this, Clint. You've got to believe that."

"I do believe that," Clint replied. "I wouldn't have come if I knew Bobby was the sort to pay to have men killed. He could have been in that line of work himself, but he was always more prone to bringing in his men alive."

With those words still hanging in the air, Clint looked in the back of the little room toward the occupied cells. Amazingly, the first prisoner was still snoring loudly, spewing out the stench of cheap whisky with every exhale. The other prisoner was crouched down against his one wall, staring intently between the bars.

"Who were those men?" Clint asked.

O'Connover shrugged. "I didn't get a look at their faces."

The apathetic tone in O'Connover's voice didn't set too well with Clint. In fact, it made his blood run hot as it raced through his veins.

"Oh, you didn't get a good look?" Clint asked. "Here, let me take care of that."

Clint spun on his heels and stormed toward the front door. He flung the door open, slamming it against the wall, and headed straight toward the body of the man wearing the blue bandanna. The man was bulky and heavier now that life had left him, but Clint's anger was enough to make up for the difference.

He hefted the corpse and dragged it into the jailhouse. Taking hold of the back of Blue's shirt as though he were picking up a dog by the scruff of its neck, Clint lifted the body and pressed it against the bars. With his free hand, Clint pulled the bandanna away from the dead man's face and pushed it even harder against the iron.

"How about that?" Clint snarled. "Take a good look, O'Connover, and tell me what you see. Are you looking at him?"

O'Connover was visibly shaken, and he pushed himself against the wall in an attempt to get even farther away from Clint.

"Tell me, O'Connover. Are you getting a good look?"

O'Connover squeaked something but didn't make any sense.

"What was that?"

"I said I'm looking!" O'Connover finally shouted.

"Who is he? One of your boys?"

"I've seen him before, but I don't know his name!"

"Don't bullshit me."

"I swear to God," O'Connover sputtered. "I swear on my father's grave, I don't know his name!"

The anger was no longer flaring inside of him, but Clint kept the intensity on his face all the same. He could tell that O'Connover was telling the truth. Either that, or he was a hell of a lot stronger than Clint had given him credit for.

"They'll keep coming for him," LeAnne said. "There may be more of them waiting for us right now."

Outside, Clint could already hear the sound of people starting to emerge from their hiding places, talking to each other in quick, excited tones. Although the firefight had been quick, Clint knew it was just a matter of luck that a stray round hadn't found its place in the body of some man, woman or child standing in the wrong place at the wrong time.

"Did you hear me?" LeAnne asked. "I said there could be more of them."

"I heard you. I also agree. That's why we've got to get this man out of town before someone gets hurt." Glancing first at Blue's dead face and then over to O'Connover, he added, "Someone that didn't call down the thunder themselves, that is."

With that, Clint released his grip on Blue's collar and let the body slide down the bars and drop onto the floor. The corpse hit with a solid thump that shook throughout the entire room and ended with Blue gazing up at O'Connover through glazed-over eyes.

"We'll be right back," Clint said. "I'll just leave you here with your friend until then."

Clint left the body where it had fallen and headed for the door. LeAnne followed but only after running her hands over the body and searching each and every pocket. Finding nothing but a pouch of tobacco, she took the gun belt from around Blue's waist and slung it over her shoulder.

Without breaking stride, Clint bent down to pick up Blue's pistol as he passed the spot where it had landed outside. He stuck the gun beneath his belt and listened for the sound of LeAnne stepping outside and locking the jailhouse behind her.

The inside of the little building was quiet as a tomb. Every so often, the grunting, wheezing snore of the drunk in the cell next to O'Connover's rumbled through the air.

NINE

Clint didn't go far after leaving the jailhouse. Keeping his eye on the people making their way along the street, he picked out a spot with a good view of the jail as well as the body in front of it and waited. Although a little rattled, LeAnne stepped up beside him and stood quietly while she caught her breath.

Before too long, she asked, "Are we waiting for more of them to come at us?"

"Not exactly," Clint said. "If there are more, they'll come after us in time no matter what we do. We've got a while before the others find out about this. If there are more gun hands nearby, they'll need to take a little time to figure out what to do now that two of their own won't be coming back."

"All right then. That just leaves me with one question. Why are we still here?"

"You said there's some law in this town. I was thinking this would be the best time to meet him rather than make him track me down."

LeAnne let out a short laugh. "Oh, well in that case you might want to find someplace warmer because we could be waiting here a long time."

37

Rather than ask her about the town's law, Clint decided to wait and let the situation speak for itself. Sure enough, well over an hour passed before someone finally came. It wasn't a particularly busy section of town, so when a person headed toward them, it was obvious.

He was a solidly built man in his fifties wearing a thick coat, hat and gloves. After tipping his hat to Clint and LeAnne, he walked straight past them and went over to where Red's body was lying. Standing over that body, the big man looked over to Clint and asked, "Any more?"

"There's one inside."

The big man tipped his hat again, went into the jailhouse and emerged with Blue's body slung over his shoulders. "I'll be back to collect the other one," he said before walking right back from where he'd come.

"That wasn't the law, was it?" Clint asked, already fairly certain of the answer.

LeAnne shook her head. "Nope."

"All right, then. I think I've seen plenty. Let's go warm up."

They both left their spots and headed back to the main street. Certainly the undertaker wouldn't mind not having an audience when he came back to collect his second customer for the day.

"All right, Bobby," Clint said once he, LeAnne and Bobby Hill were all gathered in a little saloon on the edge of town. "I'll take the job."

Bobby's face lit up and he jumped from his chair to extend his hand toward Clint. "Really? That's great news!"

"I owe you one, don't I?" Clint said, shaking Bobby's hand. "Besides, it's been a while since I've been that far north. Granted, I would have picked a better time to travel that way, but sometimes you've just got to play the cards you're dealt."

"You won't regret this, Clint. I swear I'll make this worth your while." Suddenly, some of the fire in Bobby's eyes sputtered out and he swallowed hard. "There'll be more men like that coming after O'Connover. I'm certain of it. I couldn't live with myself if you got hurt while—"

"And I couldn't live with myself if I left knowing someone else would get hurt in my place," Clint interrupted. "I still don't know all the angles here and I'm pretty sure you don't know them either."

Bobby's reaction to Clint's statement confirmed the Gunsmith's suspicion. Bobby lowered his eyes again and let out a troubled breath. He had the look of a man who'd held onto a bluffing hand for too long and was one bet away from losing everything he owned.

"I'm in over my head here," Bobby admitted. "I should've known better when there was so much money involved, but I just couldn't pass it up. Not when O'Connover just fell into my lap like that."

Clint looked over to LeAnne and saw her roll her eyes. Although Bobby had taken her as his partner, he obviously didn't appreciate everything she did to uphold her part of the bargain.

"I'd take him myself, but I know I'm just not up to it anymore." Bobby pulled in a deep breath and let it out. "After what happened in Dodge, I just don't have the sand for this business."

Clint walked up to Bobby, put his hand on the other man's shoulder and looked him square in the eyes. "Then I want you to make me a promise."

"Name it."

"When this job is over, you're out of this business for good."

"You got it," Bobby said a little too quickly.

"I mean it. I don't care if the most wanted man in the country strolls into your restaurant wearing handcuffs and shackles. You'll wait for someone else to pick him up. If you get offered more money than you've ever heard of to do another easy run, you'll turn it down. Is that a promise?"

This time, Bobby took a few seconds to mull over what Clint had demanded. Looking Clint straight in the eyes as well, Bobby responded in a solemn voice, "I swear it."

"All right then. That's good enough for me." Taking a step back, Clint stopped and narrowed his eyes. "And if you decide to take on one more job despite what you said here today, don't expect me to come running back here to pull your ass out of the fire."

Rather than be put off by Clint's warning tone, Bobby smiled and nodded. "Trust me, I learn for my mistakes. If I live through this one, the only time you'll hear from me again is when I invite you over for dinner."

"And don't think for one moment," Clint added, allowing his expression to lighten, "that I won't take you up on that one. Now that that's settled, let's get down to business."

TEN

The place where Clint, Bobby and LeAnne sat and talked was different than any other he'd been in since arriving in Krieger's Pass. Clint didn't realize just how different it was until the three of them sat down and started hashing out the details of the job in front of them. Unlike most other places in town, this one wasn't bucking up against some major throughway where people constantly fought for their space.

It was a little house on the edge of town that had either been built before the rest of the buildings around it or had been constructed with quiet in mind. The front door and main rooms were facing out and away from the rest of town, making it seem as though it had been constructed backward. There were not a lot of other buildings around and none that attracted any amount of patronage.

Every so often, Clint would look out the window and let out a relieved breath when he saw open land as opposed to crooked buildings and a constant flow of horses and people. Clint felt like a man who didn't know how hot the bathwater was until he got out of the tub. Having this taste of the quiet that he'd all but forgotten since his time in town, he found himself wanting nothing more than to saddle up and ride out.

He realized just then that it took a strong person to live in a place like Krieger's Pass. Not just because of the noise and transient population, but because such a town was teetering on the edge of something. Either it would boom and sprout into a more livable community, or it would tear itself apart like so many other towns had before it.

It wasn't an easy place to live once the winter started ripping into flesh and bone in full force. Judging by the drop in temperature that Clint could feel no matter how many walls or layers of clothing were between him and the wind, the cold had yet to fully bare its claws.

Apart from the three huddled around a little round table, there were only a few others inside the little shack. The place was a saloon and restaurant combined into one, but it was too small to feel more like one or the other. As such, it was a perfect setting for the private discussion Clint wanted to have about the impending journey with O'Connover in custody.

"We've got to assume that the attempts to break O'Connover out will continue," Clint said. "In fact, it's safe to say they'll get worse once we're traveling out in the open. Who else is going with us?"

"I'll be going," LeAnne said. "There's also a few others who'd be suited for the task, but I think we should keep the party small so we can travel quicker and draw less attention."

Nodding, Clint said, "Agreed. It would help to have someone along who can handle themselves in the cold. I've done my share of riding, but having an expert along would sure be nice."

"I already have two people in mind by the names of Varrell and Dunn. Between them, they've got experience ranging from trapping and hunting to living off of some

of the worst land you can imagine. If they can't survive
out there, nobody can."

"Sounds good. When do we meet up with them?"

"As soon as you want to ride. They've been waiting
around town and are itching to move out."

"Then let's not keep them waiting," Clint said. "I say
we move out tomorrow morning. With a gang of killers
fighting to get O'Connover away from us, the sooner we
get away from here the better."

Bobby took everything in while sipping from a glass
of whiskey he'd ordered. He seemed content to let Le-
Anne speak her mind but stepped in when he had something to add. "I've got someone I want to send along as
well."

LeAnne was already shaking her head. "No, you don't.
Not Ned."

"What've you got against Ned?" Bobby shot back.

Before LeAnne could respond, Clint cut in. "Who's
Ned?"

LeAnne slumped back in her chair and motioned toward Bobby as though she was giving him center stage.
"Go on then and tell him."

Bobby started to talk but was cut off when LeAnne
quickly raised her finger like she was scolding a child.
"And if I don't hear you tell him everything, I'll cut you
right to the quick, Bobby Hill."

Shaking his head with a slight roll of his eyes, Bobby
turned to Clint and said, "He's a good man, Clint, and
I'm sure you've met plenty like him before. His name's
Ned Gien and he could be one hell of a help to you when
things get rough."

"Is he a hired gun?" Clint asked.

"Not exactly." Bobby's eyes flinched over to LeAnne
before adding, "Well, he used to be, but that's all behind
him. He's handy with the iron and he knows this trade.

He also knows his way north of the border and has plenty of folks up there as well."

"By that, I'm guessing you mean on both sides of the law."

"A man in Ned's line of work had to know both to stay alive."

"I want to keep this party as small as possible, but a good man could make a difference. What about you, LeAnne? What do you think?"

"I don't trust Ned," she replied without hesitation. "Never have and never will. He can fight, though."

"You think we could use him?"

LeAnne thought about that for a minute and then grudgingly nodded. "He does know his way through Canada. After sneaking around so many years, he knows plenty of ways to slither around without being seen, I'd wager."

"Then I'm convinced," Clint said. "Ned's coming."

Bobby shook Clint's hand for what felt like the one hundred and fiftieth time. "My thanks to you, Clint. Once this is over, I'll be able to retire and even give LeAnne here enough to put this kind of work behind her as well. I don't know how I can repay you."

"After this," Clint said, "we're even. That's good enough for me."

"Well, it ain't good enough for me," Bobby replied. "You'll get your cut of the reward, and I won't hear a word about it. I've got a room or two for rent in my place, so make yourself at home there and I'll arrange to get the supplies together."

"Sounds great." Clint watched as Bobby went over some more of the job's specifics. Overall, the stout man seemed relieved and happy to be putting the job into more capable hands.

Clint had a nagging suspicion, however, that Bobby was just relieved and happy to be passing a hot potato from his hands to someone else's.

Anyone else's.

ELEVEN

It turned out that Bobby really hadn't been expecting Clint to take the job. In fact, after going through all the preparations, Clint wondered if Bobby had expected to do not much more than let O'Connover sit in that jail cell until he was broken out or simply died of old age.

Going over such practical matters as pulling together supplies and agreeing on times to leave or check in, Bobby grew increasingly excited as he realized the job was actually going to get done. Also, Clint got an even better handle on just how integral a part of the process LeAnne was. She spoke like a true professional, and when it was all said and done, Clint couldn't help but respect her that much more.

It was dark and the wind was numbingly cold by the time they were through. The entire building rattled with the winds, and when they died down, the sound of the nearby commotion could be heard. It wasn't anything to be concerned about, just the normal chaos infecting a town stuffed with too many people.

After Bobby had left to do some more arranging, Clint stepped outside and filled his lungs with fresh air that chilled him to the marrow. The cold seeped into his chest and started squeezing his heart before he let out the breath. That was more than enough to energize him after all the talking.

"Are you from around here?" LeAnne asked as she moved in beside him.

Clint looked at her and shook his head. "No. I'm from a bit farther east, but lately West Texas has been the closest thing to a home."

"You're a long ways from Texas. I figured you for more of a local seeing as how you take this cold in stride. Most folks grouse after their first shiver."

"I've gotten used to a lot of things. The trick is to find the good in whatever it is and enjoy that while recognizing the bad and keeping it at a distance."

She nodded and rubbed her hands together. "Sounds like a smart way to go about things."

"What about you?" Clint asked. "What brought you here?"

"To Oregon or to working with Bobby?"

"Both."

"My father dragged us out here when I was a baby. We lost my mother and sister along the way. Since me and my three brothers were the only ones to make it apart from my father, I was always told that I was the strongest of the bunch. Pa always said the boys were made tougher, but I must've had real sand to be the only female to survive the trip."

"Looks to me like he was right about that. I haven't seen many women in your line of work."

"Well," she said with a shrug, "it just sort of happened. A woman can get away with a lot more in most men's eyes simply because we're all supposed to be frail and helpless. You'd be surprised how much slack a woman can buy with a few bats of her eyelashes."

That brought back a flood of memories for Clint regarding a whole lot of women he'd encountered over the

years. "Actually," he said as all those pretty faces flew
through his mind, "I wouldn't be surprised in the least.
But you don't seem to be like that, and somehow I have
a hard time picturing you batting your eyelashes at anyone."

LeAnne laughed. The sound was warm and inviting
even though it created a chilling mist as it escaped from
her mouth. "Yeah, well I only save that for special oc-
casions. Seeing how we first met up, I'm surprised you
think I can even keep my head on straight."

"Sure, and seeing as how I almost got trampled a few
times myself just getting from one place to another around
here, I can't fault you for doing the same." For a few
minutes, Clint stood quietly, letting the cold settle into
him. Then, without taking his eyes from the glittering
stars in the sky, he said, "Tell me about Ned Gien."

"There's not much else to say. I don't trust him, but
Bobby apparently does so that's all that matters."

"No, it isn't. Bobby's not the one riding through all
that snow and ice. We are. And if we're going to be riding
with someone I can't trust, then I want to know about it."

"I thought you were fine with taking him along."

"Bobby was already set on the idea. Fighting him about
it would have taken up time that we can't afford to lose.
We can make a decision anytime about this, unless it's
already too late." Taking hold of her by the shoulders in
a gentle, yet insistent way, Clint looked her in the eyes
and asked, "Is there anything else you want to say·about
him?"

For a moment, it looked as though LeAnne was going
to go along with what had already been decided. Then she
paused and thought it over. Finally, she shook her head
and replied, "Honestly, I've never seen him do anything
against me or Bobby. He's got a past, but I've done some
things myself that don't hold up too well under close in-
spection."

"Is he a man we can trust to pull us through this?"

"He fought back some of that gang himself before you arrived. He's got no reason to cross us, and with what Bobby's paying, I doubt he'll get a better offer from some bunch of outlaws. So I guess my answer is that we bring him."

"There's something else you're not saying," Clint told her.

Squaring her jaw, LeAnne straightened up and said, "Ned does know plenty of ways to get over the border without being caught by anyone on either side of the law. But I'll be keeping my eye on him, and if I see him step out of line, I'll handle him myself."

This time, Clint could tell she was being up-front with him, not hiding a thing. "All right then," he said, loosening his hold. "We'd better rest up and get out of this cold."

Though his hands were no longer on her, LeAnne still drifted toward him as if Clint were pulling her in. "That's funny," she said in a softer voice. "I was just starting to feel pretty warm."

TWELVE

It was going to be a long ride to Canada. Krieger's Pass was a ways up north already, but a hell of a lot of rugged terrain and frozen air stood between Oregon and the spot that was to be Russ O'Connover's final destination. Clint knew he was in for a rough ride and so did LeAnne. For that reason alone, they both decided to make the most of their last night in town together.

They had concluded earlier that the ride would be safer if they kept away from prying eyes as much as possible. That meant camping instead of hotels. That also meant sleeping on the cold ground rather than enjoying the comfort of a pillow and blanket for the duration of the journey.

All of that was to start the next day, which was even more reason to savor the bed while they still could. Instead of going to the little room Bobby had offered, Clint was taken—or, more accurately, dragged—to LeAnne's room by a very anxious LeAnne.

On the way, they'd talked a little bit about nothing much at all, and by the time they got into the room, there wasn't one more word to be said. It was a small but comfortable room in a hotel across the street from Bobby's

Place. The window looked down onto the main street, and there was enough snow outside to reflect the light of the moon back into the room.

The pale light gave the air a cool, restful feel. As they stepped inside and shut the door, neither one wanted to make a sound for fear it would break the spell that had come over them both. For a moment, they stood in the quiet darkness, looking into each other's eyes.

Then Clint reached out for her with both hands, which was all LeAnne needed to come rushing into his embrace. She wrapped her arms around him and held him tight as she kissed him urgently and powerfully. Clint was caught up in the moment as well, his excitement growing as he allowed his hands to roam freely over LeAnne's body.

Clint's penis became rigid with the expectation of what was to come. Sensing his excitement, LeAnne reached down between his legs to massage the warm hardness to be found there. Feeling her hands stroking him through his jeans, Clint slid one hand down her back until he could cup the solid firmness of her buttocks. His other hand slid up along her side until it was filled with her soft, firm breast.

LeAnne leaned back and pulled in a deep breath, keeping her hand on Clint's erection. "Oh God," she whispered. "That feels so good."

Fighting back the shudder as LeAnne kept working up and down on his penis, Clint replied, "You have no idea."

Hearing that, LeAnne smiled broadly and placed her hands over Clint's. After allowing him to caress her a bit more, she gripped his hands and moved them away from her body. From there, she eased her hands down along his arms and then over his chest. Her fingers continued their journey downward as she lowered herself onto her knees in front of him.

Her eyes darted up to meet his as she pulled open his gun belt and then started to remove his jeans. "You thought that felt good?" she asked as her hand slipped between his legs once again to take hold of his bare cock. "Try this."

LeAnne's full lips slowly parted and the tip of her tongue emerged to greet the tip of Clint's penis as she guided it into her mouth. Her tongue slid along the bottom of the shaft, and her lips didn't close around him until most of his length was in her mouth. When she did purse her lips together, she moved her tongue back and forth while sucking him gently.

The sensation Clint felt was so intense that he had to lean back against the wall for support. Clint slid his fingers through LeAnne's hair as her head bobbed back and forth with quickening strokes. Her hands had hold of his hips and her eyes were shut tightly as she worked her mouth on him even harder.

Although he could have let her do that to him all night long, Clint wanted to make her knees as weak as she was making his. When she felt him pull her head back, LeAnne sucked him hard enough to make his knees tremble before finally allowing him to leave her mouth.

"What's the matter?" she asked as she stood back up again. "You didn't like that?"

Clint was already peeling the clothes off of her. LeAnne's body was tight and firm beneath her rugged outfit. She had a way of making even the plain undershirt seem especially sexy: it clung to her pert breasts, allowing the hard nipples to show up perfectly in the moonlight.

"Oh, I liked that just fine," he said, unfastening her pants and pulling them down over her hips. "But I thought I'd like to give you a taste of it as well. Well actually," he added, picking her up and setting her down on the edge of the bed, "I'd be the one getting a taste."

LeAnne's muscled legs moved apart the instant Clint put his hands on her thighs and lowered his face down between them. Her pussy was wet and she let out a shuddering moan as soon as Clint's mouth brushed teasingly over the two pink lips.

Propping herself up on her elbows, LeAnne let her head drop back at first so she could feel the pleasure Clint was giving her wash throughout her entire body. She draped one leg over Clint's shoulder and then lifted her head again so she could watch him as he flicked his tongue over her inner thighs and started licking tiny circles over her clitoris.

LeAnne's skin felt cool against Clint's tongue, which made the warmth inside of her feel even hotter by comparison. While rubbing his hands up and down along her legs, Clint kissed her and licked her until he could feel her entire body squirming against his face.

She clawed at the bed and clenched her fists over the sheets as the movement of Clint's tongue on her pussy brought her over the brink and into an orgasm. When she climaxed, every muscle in her body stiffened and didn't relax again until some of the intense pleasure started to fade.

"Come here," she ordered in a rugged whisper. "I can't wait another second."

Clint felt her hands take hold of him, pulling at his shoulders or arms or whatever she could reach. Allowing himself to be led by her insistent fingers, Clint got onto the bed and lowered himself down on top of her. LeAnne eagerly opened her legs wide and wrapped them around him while guiding his rigid cock into her pussy with one hand.

When he pushed his hips forward and buried himself inside of her, Clint thought he could have been buck naked in the middle of the arctic and still not have felt a bit of cold. The warmth of her skin combined with the heat of being inside of her rushed through his entire body. LeAnne felt the same thing and let out a deep breath while her body relaxed to accept him.

They both rocked back and forth on the bed as Clint moved in and out of her in a steady rhythm. Their eyes fixed on each other, and Clint saw instantly when he brushed up against one of her favorite spots. LeAnne's eyes widened as did her smile when he shifted his hips a certain way and pumped into her. Once he'd found that spot, Clint stayed there and slid his hand along the side of her breast, down to her tight buttocks and back again.

Reaching up to clench her fists around the sheets once again, LeAnne closed her eyes tightly and let her body go wherever Clint wanted to take her. The cool moonlight spilled over her naked skin, bathing her flesh in a luminescence as she stretched out beneath Clint's body.

They made love until they were both spent, after which they fell asleep in each other's arms. She woke him up in the dead of night by slipping beneath the covers and sucking him until he was hard again.

"We've got a long ride ahead of us," she said when he looked down at her with pleasant surprise. "I aim to use this bed for every bit that it's worth."

They certainly did just that.

And then some more.

THIRTEEN

Clint and LeAnne met with Bobby and the rest of the party at dawn. It hadn't taken much to pull together the others riding with them because that group had been waiting around for the go-ahead for some time. The only challenge for Bobby was in gathering up all the horses and equipment needed for the group's trek into the snowy northern expanses.

The day was especially bright: every ray of light reflected off the iced-over snow. The snow, in turn, appeared brilliantly white, bathing in the sunlight that practically stuck to the glassy surface.

Clint had to shield his eyes from the brightness of the day as he and LeAnne walked up to join their assembled party. They were all gathered at the stable on the edge of town, the same stable where Eclipse had eventually wound up. The sun was just shining through in full force, but Bobby was pacing as if he'd been waiting in that spot the better part of the night.

"There you are, you two," Bobby said as he stomped over to greet Clint and LeAnne. "Did you stop off for a leisurely breakfast?"

"No," Clint said, trying not to be too obvious about

what he was thinking. "Just making sure we got enough rest."

The distracted look in Bobby's eyes suggested he either didn't have the faintest clue why Clint and LeAnne had arrived at the same time or he simply didn't care. "Well, did you get enough sleep?"

LeAnne smacked Bobby on the rump and headed straight for the rest of the group. "Tossing and turning all night long, but it was a hell of a night."

"Glad to see you're in such high spirits," Bobby said. "I, on the other hand, didn't get a wink of rest."

Just then a man around Clint's height stepped forward and pushed back a thick chunk of long hair that had fallen over his face. "You're not the one that needs the rest. You'll be sleeping under all them blankets of yours just as warm as you please while the rest of us are freezing our balls off." Glancing toward LeAnne, he tipped his hat and said, "Or whatever else it is you can freeze off."

"Always the gentleman," LeAnne said with undisguised contempt. Turning to Clint, she said, "Clint Adams, this is Ned Gien."

Ned was dressed in layers of shabby coats the color of frozen mud. His hands were covered by tattered gloves, the pieces of which he'd barely sewn together. Extending a hand toward Clint, he showed a wide smile that displayed more than a few chipped teeth.

"Always a pleasure to meet a legend," Ned said.

When Clint shook Ned's hand, he felt a definite strength in the other man's bony grip. The glove shifted over Ned's hand, revealing a few more busted stitches and ragged seams.

"Heard a lot about you, Ned," Clint replied.

Ned's icy eyes shifted over toward LeAnne. "Yeah. I'll just bet you have."

There were a few others standing clustered around a small wagon that looked more like a cart with a squared roof. Two men stood there; one was a burly mountain-man type, and the other was a slender youth whose skin looked tougher than leather.

To the burly fellow, Clint said, "I suppose you're the one that'll dig that wagon out when the rest of us are too frozen to move."

The big man smiled at Clint's teasing tone and nodded. "I would be happy to help. That is, if you need it between here and a few miles outside of town."

"No offense meant," Clint added. "I was just—"

"He's not going," Bobby cut in. "He's the stableman. He was nice enough to bring the horses around so early this morning."

"Looks like you'll have to dig yourself out, then," the big fellow said with a wink.

Now that he'd had most of his good humor crumpled up and tossed aside, Clint turned a wary eye to the others that remained by the cart. "I thought you said you'd provide us with some help, Bobby."

"I did," Bobby replied as he rushed up to Clint's side. "There's Ned and LeAnne. They're damn good hunters and scouts right there. I gave ya Mike Dunn," he said, pointing toward the lanky kid with the bad skin. "Besides being a born trapper, he's not too bad with a firearm."

The kid nodded once and held open his coat to reveal several pistols and even a sawed-off shotgun strapped to his torso and under his arms. "Any kind of firearm, Mister Adams," he said in a voice that sounded like two rusted spikes being scraped together.

Beaming proudly, Bobby said, "And to top it off, I convinced the best damn tracker I ever seen to ride with ya."

Clint had briefly noticed the figure leaning against the cart the moment he and LeAnne had arrived. But because that same figure was wrapped head to toe in coats and scarves, Clint had yet to see one bit of skin or even a facial feature. In fact, the figure had been so still the entire time, he'd damn near overlooked the person completely.

Now the figure started to move, and Clint became fully aware of this person who'd been right in front of him the whole time. Watching the way the person moved, Clint couldn't possibly miss the fact that the figure belonged to a woman.

She was tall and slender, moving with the grace and confidence of a cat. She not only knew that she hadn't truly been seen, but also prided herself on it. Extending a gloved hand, she gave Clint a strong smile. "Pleased to meet you, Mister Adams. My name's Sandra Varrell. I'm glad to be working with you."

Clint couldn't help but be transfixed by the dark depth of her eyes. He let his gaze linger for a moment and then pulled himself back on track. "Likewise. I guess that only leaves one more," he added, pointing toward the cart, which had started shifting slightly back and forth.

Turning to pull open the small square door leading to the back of the cart, Sandra said, "I think you two have already met."

Clint didn't know how it had been done, but Russ O'Connover was scrunched up inside the cart. He was hog-tied and lying amid supplies and provisions that took up more space than he did.

"Is this all?" Clint asked, looking around to the small group and poor excuse for a wagon.

Bobby seemed proud of the bunch and nodded. "Yep."

"Then we might as well get going. The sooner we start, the sooner this'll all be over."

FOURTEEN

"There they go." Sitting on top of a mare that was almost light enough in color to blend in with the dirty snow, a man with a square jaw and stoic features peered through a spyglass toward Krieger's Pass. His voice had a German hue to it, and the smile on his face could be heard in his statement.

Sure enough, when he lowered the spyglass, the man smirked and handed the telescope to the man beside him. The second man was also on horseback but somehow seemed much smaller than the first. Taking the spyglass, he lifted the lens to his eye and looked through it.

"What about O'Connover?" the second man asked. "Is he with them?"

"He is. They loaded him into that cart before sunrise. Ol' Bobby probably thought he was being sneaky."

The second man's face was covered in whiskers. Those whiskers, in turn, were coated with soup from the last eight meals and squirmed on his face as he scowled while squinting through the telescope. "I recognize Ned and that sweet little blonde. I think I seen that kid before, but I don't know about them others."

"The man toward the front on the Darley Arabian is

Clint Adams. The woman with him is probably just along for the ride or is acting as some kind of guide."

The second man lowered the spyglass and looked over at the bigger man with wide eyes. "Clint Adams? The Gunsmith? You sure about that, Burt?"

Burt nodded slowly. As he watched the party roll out of the cramped town, the veins in his thick neck stood out beneath his collar. "Of course I'm sure. Word got out that Adams was in San Francisco about a month ago, and I went to see for myself since we were down that way anyhow."

"It could still be someone just claiming to be Adams."

"It's him, Frye."

The smaller man knew better than to question Burt when he took on that particular tone. The big man's voice got an edge to it that struck the same chord in a man as the sound of a gun being cocked directly behind him.

"All right, it's him," Frye said. "Now what?"

"The plan's the same now as it ever was. The only difference is that O'Connover's not locked up in a jail cell anymore."

"They're pointed north. That means they're probably making a run for Canada."

"Probably."

Burt had yet to take his eyes away from the small group making its way out of town. With his eyelids already narrow slits, the only part of him that moved were the steely orbs beneath those lids. When he exhaled and the air emerged as wisps of smoke from his nostrils, the effect was startling: it seemed as though a statue had just taken a breath.

"So, what are we going to do?"

"We'll let them run," Burt replied. "For now. They won't get far."

"Should we follow 'em?"

"Give them a little head start. Once they're in the open

where nobody else can help them, we'll take them. Go tell the others."

Frye nodded and brought his horse around in the opposite direction from which he'd been facing. Back that way, another group on horseback waited, a group double, if not triple, the size of the party leaving Krieger's Pass.

FIFTEEN

The ride out of town was slow and easy. Plenty of bodies still shuffled about, filling practically every available bit of space on or around the streets, but Clint's mind was at ease because he knew he would be out of that commotion in a matter of minutes. He was well acquainted with the comforts of town life, but being in Krieger's Pass was akin to sitting in a shipping crate being dragged behind a wild horse.

Towns like that bred trouble simply because most folks didn't take to that kind of living. In a world with so much open country and such wide skies, it went against a man's nature to be cooped up in such a place.

Riding out of there, Clint wondered what he might find if he came back a year or two later. Krieger's Pass could become a booming city, but it could just as easily become a memory, nothing left but broken buildings and two empty streets. In that way, towns were a lot like people: only the strong survived.

The rest, as harsh as it may be, were weeded out by a world that was too tough for them anyhow. It was a system elegant in its simple brutality. It was a system that had been around long before men had even stepped foot on the earth, and it would be there long after the last footprint had been washed away.

"You look like something's bothering you," LeAnne said while riding the horse next to him. "Is something wrong?"

Clint shook his head and pulled in a breath of frigid air. "Nah. Just thinking."

"If you're thinking that you're glad to be out of that damn town, then I was thinking the same thing myself." She twisted in her saddle to take a look at the clump of crooked buildings and the black smoke curling up from the chimneys. "It's only a matter of time before that whole place either falls down or burns down, and whichever it is, I don't want to be around for it. What about you, Mikey? You glad to be out of there?"

The youngest of the group drove the cart and hadn't said more than a word or two after introducing himself to Clint. Hearing the question, he didn't even bother lifting his eyes from the back of the horse pulling the cart. "I guess."

"You done much traveling?" LeAnne asked.

The answer didn't come from the sullen young man, but from the man who rode alongside the cart and just a bit behind.

"He's never been out of this town," Ned replied as though he'd been the one LeAnne was talking to. "Just take a look at him now and you can see that plain enough."

"I've been out of Krieger's Pass," Mike said in his own defense. "I was born up north of here a few miles and lived there for a while until they started building here."

"Oh, you were born outside of town were you?"

"Yeah. My daddy was a miner and trapper."

"And you lived out in a camp somewhere until rolling into the big bad town of Krieger's Pass?"

Mike's eyes darted between the horse in front of him

and Ned behind him. He didn't seem to pick up on the sarcastic tone in Ned's voice. Even glancing around to the rest of the party didn't help him much. Finally, he nodded in Ned's direction and said, "It wasn't a camp, though. It was a cabin my daddy built for us."

"Oh," Ned grunted. "Then excuse me all to hell."

LeAnne shot a look over her shoulder that could have melted a hole through metal. "Shut up, Ned. Leave him alone."

Ned grinned widely; it was the kind of expression a hyena wore just before he started ripping his dinner apart. "Fine, fine, I'll let the boy go. After all, I wouldn't want to piss off such a worldly, dangerous fella like that one."

"No," Clint said in a low, even tone as he turned to look Ned's way. "You wouldn't."

Hearing that, Ned let his smile fade somewhat and shut his mouth.

LeAnne gave Mike a reassuring nod and then flicked her reins so she could catch up to Clint. Although she didn't say anything to him, LeAnne gave Clint a little smirk that was more than enough to tell him she appreciated him stepping in.

At the head of the group, Sandra rode a lean white mare. The animal's flesh was the color of the ground they rode, right down to the occasional flecks of brown and black. So far, she hadn't spoken much. She'd been busy scanning the horizon and giving each step the same amount of deliberation.

Clint studied the way she moved and the way she rode. All the while, he thought about how she'd blended almost perfectly into her surroundings when they'd first met. He still had a hard time believing that he'd overlooked her like that, but now that he watched the calculating way she did every last thing, he couldn't help but hand it to her. She was good at what she did, and there was no shame in being tricked by a master.

That didn't mean, however, that he had any intention of allowing himself to be fooled a second time.

LeAnne's warm expression became as cold as the air around her when she saw Clint snap Eclipse's reins and bring the Darley Arabian up closer to Sandra. The blonde didn't try to stop him, but she made sure to watch him like a hawk.

"So you're the tracker in the group?" Clint asked.

"That's the rumor."

"How long have you been doing this kind of work?"

Sandra looked over to him and showed him a pretty yet cautious smile. "Does it matter?"

"I like to know who I'm riding with, especially since things are bound to get rough."

Nodding, Sandra turned her eyes back to the trail ahead of her and said, "I do just fine, Mister Adams. If I didn't, I wouldn't have signed up for a job that might get as rough as this one. And if that's not enough for you, perhaps you might want to take the lead out here?"

Already, Clint could sense that Sandra had not only confidence but an underlying strength as well. He admired that in anyone. "Didn't mean to ruffle any feathers," he said. "Just looking out for everyone's best interests."

"Oh by all means, keep watching over me." Leaning over so Clint could hear her when she dropped her voice to a whisper, she added, "I think that's sweet."

Knowing that he'd been dismissed, Clint moved Eclipse back into the middle of the group and let Sandra do what she'd been hired to do.

SIXTEEN

Once Krieger's Pass was behind them, there wasn't much talk among the group. Clint and LeAnne held their position in the middle of the party while Sandra remained at the head. For his part, Ned shifted his position every hour or so, resulting in him circling the wagon the way a buzzard might circle a carcass.

Mike watched silently from the driver's seat of the cart. Every so often he would flick the reins to push along the single horse pulling the wagon. Ever since he'd had words with Ned, Mike seemed even less anxious to talk than he had before. For that matter, nobody seemed too anxious to say much of anything.

Clint had plenty on his mind to keep him occupied. Now that he was out of the cramped quarters of that town, he felt he could think more clearly. Perhaps it was the combination of the fresh air and bracing cold that focused his senses. Then again, maybe it was the fact that he knew they might be ambushed at any moment.

The hours dragged by and Clint felt every second of them pass. With all the attention he was paying to the land around them as well as the people he was with, Clint had been ticking off practically every minute. Although that made him feel better about moving ahead, it sure didn't make for a fast day.

It was well past noon, but it still looked like early morning. The snow had a way of making the light seem just as bright later in the day as it was at the beginning. The glare off the frozen treetops and snow-covered hills made it difficult to see and painful to track the source of the light, which was shining like a lantern in Clint's face. The strangest part of it was that no matter how bright the sun shone, it didn't do one bit of good in keeping any of them warm.

If being in town had been good for anything at all, it was that it had helped take the edge off the bitter cold. Even the crooked buildings of Krieger's Pass had served as a good shelter from the wind. Out on the open trail, riding under the stark blue sky and brilliant sun, the members of the party felt as if they had ice water in their veins. Not one of them, however, was going to be the first to complain about it.

Clint noticed the moment Sandra's head perked up. The motion caught his eye because it was the first time she'd lifted her nose from the trail since their conversation earlier in the day. Looking left and right in two quick snaps of her head, she held up an open hand, giving the signal for Mike to stop the cart.

"What's wrong?" Clint asked, bringing Eclipse alongside Sandra's mare. Although he wanted to get her attention, he didn't want to block the view of whatever it was that she had seen.

Ned was circling around to their right, and he stopped when he was turned around and facing the entire party. "Yeah. What's wrong, Sandy?" He asked in a taunting tone.

"Get back there by the cart," Sandra said to Ned.

"Why? Did you finally see those men that've been following us?"

"What?" Clint asked, turning to look at Ned and then at the surrounding land. "What men?"

Pulling in a deep breath through her nose, Sandra said, "A group of them. Could be pretty big."

Clint was still looking around, trying to pick out what the hell Sandra and Ned were talking about. So far, he couldn't see much. But then again, the landscape started to waver and blur in the glare of the sun off the snow about fifty yards out. The wind howled through his ears like a constant rush of water.

"I still don't see anything," Clint said out of frustration.

Ned let out a slow breath. "They're still out there. Wouldn't you agree, Sandy?"

Turning toward Clint, she gave him a deadly serious look and nodded. "Yes. I agree."

"Goddammit," Clint said under his breath. "How come I haven't seen them?"

"Because you're not used to this stretch of land and you don't know these parts as well as we do," Sandra answered. "Besides, it's not your job to know these things. It's mine."

Sandra had a few good points, but that didn't make Clint any happier about being the last to know something so important. Keeping himself facing the same direction as Sandra had been looking, Clint dug in his saddlebag until his hand touched a familiar piece of dented metal.

He pulled out the spyglass and extended it with a flick of his wrist. He held it to his eye but was immediately blinded by a flash of white glare, which was amplified by the focusing glass.

Ned was looking at him with a disbelieving smirk and shaking his head. "You might not want to do that just yet, Adams. It takes a while to get used to being out here."

"I've gotten used to a whole lot of things worse than this," Clint replied. When he looked through the glass a second time, Clint was more careful to take the factors of his environment into consideration. It wasn't that he hadn't known to before. It was just that he felt hurried to keep moving—his joints threatened to grind to a halt if they stayed still too long.

With one hand, Clint brought the telescope up to his eye. With the other, he shielded the end of the spyglass from the intense sunlight. The contrast of white snow against the darker forms of trees and exposed soil played tricks with him more than once. Finally, Clint spotted some movement that was neither a trick of the light nor a rustle of the wind.

"That could be them, I guess," Clint said. "It's impossible to say how many of them there are, though."

"How about you let us go scout it out, then?" Ned suggested.

Clint hesitated and looked over to Sandra. She was looking back at him, waiting for an answer as well.

"I think I should go with you," Clint finally said.

Shaking her head, Sandra said, "Not with me. I move too quickly."

"Yeah, but I just—"

Ned brought his horse around and started riding away from the group. "How about this? Mikey over there gets this wagon moving again while you and LeAnne ride along with it. Fan out so you can make it look like there's more of us here, and Sandra and I will catch up with you before you even know we're gone."

Clint made no attempt to hide his disapproval. "I didn't agree to take orders from you, Ned."

"And I didn't agree to take none from you, either. We're all in this together. No one here is doubting why you were hired, so what gives you the right to start doubting us?"

"I don't have my doubts about everyone," Clint said. "Just you."

Ned brought his horse up close to Eclipse and glared

straight into Clint's eyes. "You've been listening to that blonde of yours too much."

"Why you son of a—" LeAnne started to say, but she stopped when she saw that the other two weren't even looking at her.

"Every man needs to prove himself," Clint said. "I'm sure I've got to do the same thing in your eyes."

"All right then. That's fair enough," Ned said as he turned his horse back toward the ridge that Clint had been studying through the spyglass. "But if you do one thing to give away my position, then I'll knock you out and pick you up on my way back."

Clint nodded at that. "You got yourself a deal."

The two men rode away from the group, leaving LeAnne and Mike to roll on with their prisoner.

Sandra had already slipped away without leaving a trace behind her.

SEVENTEEN

Clint and Ned broke away from the others as if slowly branching off to scout the trail ahead. Although he was worried he may have been seen staring toward those who were following them, Clint had seen only a few shapes far off in the distance. Since he hadn't spotted any eyes looking back at him when he looked through his spyglass, Clint reckoned those others couldn't see much of his group either.

It was a small comfort, especially considering what was at stake if he was wrong. But Clint was willing to take any comfort he could get. One other thing that nagged at him was the fact that he'd completely lost track of Sandra again. It was as though she'd simply disappeared, and Clint was not accustomed to being so unaware of someone so close to him.

He couldn't allow that to distract him, however. For the time being, Clint needed to focus all of his faculties on the task at hand as well as on the man helping him with that task. Ned had stopped talking after they'd broken away from the group, communicating instead with simple hand gestures. Pointing first toward a stand of trees

71

about eighty yards away, Ned steered his horse in that direction.

Either Ned figured Clint would follow, or he didn't care. That much was obvious. He didn't bother to check on Clint as they circled around the trees. And once the trees were between them and the group they'd spotted, Ned touched his heels to his horse's sides and raced toward the shelter of the foliage.

The trees were mostly pines, so the cluster provided an excellent screen. After pulling back hard on his reins, Ned slowed his horse to a near stop and swung down from his saddle. He hit the ground running and dashed for the biggest, closest tree he could find. Clint performed a similar maneuver, but Eclipse stopped as soon as his saddle was empty whereas Ned's horse continued wandering toward the trees.

It wasn't until Clint took a closer look that he saw Ned's horse was actually tethered to one of the trees inside the screen of cover. A soft whistle was all Clint needed to bring Eclipse to him and within the protection of the pines as well.

Ned glanced over his shoulder and spotted Clint. He pointed to himself and to the left before pointing at Clint and then to the right. Acknowledging the command with a nod, Clint kept low and headed to the right while Ned went in the opposite direction.

As he made his way through the trees, Clint tried to keep track of Ned. It wasn't easy. Whenever he took his eyes away from his own path, Clint was able to catch only fleeting glimpses of Ned. That made sense considering that Ned, like Clint, was trying to stay out of sight, but it still didn't set well with Clint.

It was in Clint's nature to want to know as much as possible about every card on the table. Dealing with the wild ones tended to throw things out of whack by introducing factors that could not be predicted or controlled.

For the time being, however, he would have to deal with the situation at hand and make due with his transient sightings of Ned.

Finally, Clint reached the other side of the trees and peered out at the familiar sight of the little cart being pulled by a lone horse. He could see LeAnne riding near the cart.

Clint's ears picked up the rustle of a few leaves and when he turned, he saw Ned settling in right next to him. The sight of the other man so unexpectedly close brought Clint's hand reflexively to the Colt at his side. He didn't draw the weapon, but he left his hand there to make sure Ned saw how close he'd come to getting a bad surprise of his own.

"Take it easy, Adams," Ned said in a whisper that blended almost perfectly into the wind. "There's nobody in here but us."

"Are you certain about that?"

"I checked my half. Didn't you check yours?"

"You want to check something? Why don't you check the horizon over where you and Sandra supposedly saw that army coming at us."

Ned got down on one knee and took a long look in that direction. After only a few seconds, he nodded and said, "There they are. Not exactly an army, but big enough to give us something to think about."

Clint was looking in that direction as well, but didn't see anything until Ned spoke. Squinting into the distance, he spotted a row of riders that looked more like a row of crows lined up on a telegraph wire.

Holding his spyglass to his eye, Clint said, "They're still a ways off. That is, if that's the only group."

"I doubt there's too many more of them. Otherwise, they wouldn't have any reason not to just swoop down and overpower us."

"Yeah, but they outnumber us already."

"That doesn't mean they got the balls to face us head on. Usually men like that need that army you mentioned to muster up the nerve to throw down against the likes of you."

Clint turned to look at Ned. "You think they know I'm here?"

"Probably," Ned replied, still studying the horizon. "They seem to know a lot about what's been going on so far. It'd be safe to assume they know about you as well. Besides, if they don't know, that just makes it easier for us."

Clint had been thinking along those same lines, too. The best strategy in any situation is to plan for the worst. That way, if you're wrong, you're pleasantly surprised.

This entire time, Clint had been watching and waiting for Ned to do something to prove himself untrustworthy. That something hadn't happened. At that moment, Clint realized he'd made the mistake of accepting someone else's preconceived opinion rather than forming his own. He could have blamed LeAnne for putting that opinion in his head, but truthfully he was the one to blame for allowing himself to be influenced.

"Well, since those are the ones we can see," Clint said, "perhaps we should try to find any others that we haven't spotted yet. If they're watching us, they probably already sent out someone to see where you, me and Sandra got off to."

Ned smirked. "You're right about looking for another batch of riders. But as far as Sandra goes, I wouldn't worry about her. I'm sure she's doing just fine."

EIGHTEEN

So far, Sandra had picked out at least seven riders. Five of them were lined up like Indians staring down a wagon train, while the other two were doing their best at skirting around to flank LeAnne and the cart. Sandra had to hand it to those other two. They were doing a hell of a job. Their only problem was that they weren't as good at sneaking as Sandra was at tracking.

The signs the other two had left were fresh, which actually made them a little trickier to pick up. To the inexperienced eye, dust or powdery snow swirling in the air could mean a gust of wind or a stampeding animal. But Sandra's eyes saw things differently and she spotted the telltale signs of men on horseback. Her ears were also finely tuned enough to pick out the beating of hooves coming from directions other than that of the five riders standing in plain sight.

Sandra kept a stable of horses and had trained each of them herself. Which horse she used depended on the job she was on and where she would be going. For this job, she'd selected her horse that would blend in most with its surroundings. The animal's white, speckled coat allowed it to meld nicely with the snowy woods, and the training she'd given it allowed it to walk almost as quietly as its rider.

Once she saw that she was getting close to the source of the noise she'd heard, Sandra flicked her reins while pulling on them slightly and pressing her knees against the horse's sides. That was the signal for it to slow to a stealthy crawl, which was exactly what it did. One more tug on the reins brought the animal to a stop, its breathing not much more than a whisper.

Sandra remained perfectly still. Her eyes were open but not seeing much because all of her attention was focused on what she could hear. In seconds, she picked out the sounds she'd been searching for and in another second, she turned her head to face the precise direction from which those sounds had come.

By her calculations, there was a rider approaching from her right and ahead of her by less than a hundred yards. After taking a quick survey of her surroundings, she steered her horse toward a steep slope and dismounted.

She made a few soft, comforting sounds to her animal and pulled its reins straight down. The horse took those directions as well as it had the others and lowered itself down so it was lying on its belly with all four legs tucked beneath it. Placing a hand on the horse's head, Sandra patted the animal's mane and pushed slightly until the horse lowered its head as well. When it was done, the horse was lying much like a dog curled up at its master's bed. It was an odd sight but the horse's curious pose served its purpose very well indeed.

Sandra held her head just high enough over the top of the slope so she could see beyond it. A few seconds later, she heard the rumble of approaching hooves and then saw the rider break through a stand of trees.

Compared to the care she'd taken in her arrival, this rider might as well have tied cowbells to his saddle and fired his gun in the air as he went. He kept himself low over his animal's back, but what pains he took to cover ground without being seen didn't do a bit of good.

Sandra waited until the last possible moment to lower her head, holding off until she felt her instincts screaming for her to move. Only then did she pull her head down and press the side of her face against the ground. As if watching her, Sandra's horse tensed itself, too, as the hoof beats drew closer and closer.

Finally, the thunder reached its peak and the rider exploded over the top of the ridge. For one terrible instant, Sandra felt as though the animal was going to come down right on top of her. But instead of feeling the impact of hooves breaking her spine, she felt only the rush of air as the other rider sailed completely over both her and her horse.

Sandra twisted on the ground to watch the animal fly over her head. After what felt like an eternity of being a few inches away from being trampled, the other horse touched down and kept right on riding. Letting out the breath she'd been holding, Sandra reached out to give her own horse a couple comforting pats on the nose.

They both kept low and quiet, Sandra watching where the other one was headed and how fast he was riding. Finally, she gave the animal the signal to get back to its feet and once it was standing, she climbed into the saddle herself.

Nobody else was coming in the rider's wake, which meant she had one more man to find and precious little time in which to find him.

Sandra hadn't seen the other rider for several minutes. Although she'd broken away from Clint and the others with time to spare, after tracking the two others one at a time, she was left without much slack. It was too early to engage the gang just yet, but that didn't mean she'd be content to let them just ride up and take their shots at her group.

Using her knowledge of which direction the second rider had been headed and adding a few educated guesses, Sandra outflanked the flanker, putting herself in the path of the second rider moments before he arrived. She thought she might have been spotted, but there was nothing she could do about it now. Instead, she plowed ahead with her own plan, knowing that to give an inch might give away everything they had.

She hated to leave her horse, but Sandra got the animal to run in a straight line after she'd dropped off its back in a smooth, fluid motion. Hopefully, the other man hadn't seen her dismount, because that could very well mean the difference between life and death.

Just as Sandra had figured, the other rider snapped his reins and raced straight for Sandra's horse. He didn't think to look down as his horse jumped over a fallen log. He also didn't see Sandra's hand reached up from where she'd been lying with her back pressed against the other side of that log.

Sandra gripped a knife in her hand, raising it with the blade facing out so the horse could drag its legs across the sharpened steel. She shut her eyes and felt a clench in her stomach as she heard the horse let out a pained whinny before its front legs dropped onto the ground.

Although the horse landed well enough at first, the instant its hind legs touched down, its entire body buckled and blood sprayed from the fresh cuts just above its hooves. The rider let out a mix of curses that were lost amid the horse's cries and the desperate scrape of the animal's hooves against the earth.

Sandra winced when she heard the sounds coming from the back of the horse's throat. Its rider was trapped beneath the big animal's weight, but she fixed her eyes on the horse's face instead of the human who was hollering just as loudly.

The horse tried get up but couldn't quite manage with the cuts on its hind legs. Racing forward with knife in hand, Sandra was on the rider before he knew what was going on. She knocked him out with a sharp rap from her knife handle to his temple and then quickly pulled the gun from his holster so she could toss it away.

From there, she sifted through the saddlebags and then went back to the rider. This time, when she approached him, she came at him with the business end of her knife bared. A few quick slashes and she had shredded away his midsection.

She was done in no time and was gone the moment she jumped back into her own saddle.

NINETEEN

"She's good," Clint said as he maintained his watch through the spyglass.

Ned was lying on his belly, watching the lone rider approaching the cart. It had been only a few minutes since they'd taken up their positions, but plenty had happened in that short amount of time. "What happened?" he asked.

"I caught a glimpse of her cutting off that second fellow and now there's no trace of him."

"What about her?"

"I see her. At least, I think I see her. It's hard to tell between the color of that horse and how fast she moves." After studying the scene a few more seconds, Clint nodded. "One thing's for certain, whatever I see right now sure isn't that other fellow. She is damn good."

"Well, she must've figured we could handle this one that's still coming. He's headed straight for us."

Shifting his spyglass away from the rider he'd been keeping tabs on, Clint looked toward the one Ned had been watching. Sure enough, the rider was barreling directly for the wooded area where they were waiting. If the rider didn't mean to come through the trees, he was going to get awfully close.

LeAnne and the cart had continued moving steadily along their route, which affected the rider's course in a way that only helped Clint and Ned.

"If he still means to flank that cart," Ned pointed out, "he'll have to skirt these trees or even go around them."

"That was the idea, wasn't it?"

"Well, it's what I would'a done."

Keeping his eyes trained on the approaching figure, Clint gauged distance and speed in the space of a few heartbeats. "I give him another minute or so before he gets here. Shave some of that off if he intends to go straight for that cart."

"Or tack some on if he means to go around these trees."

"He won't do that."

Ned shifted on his belly, taking his eyes off the other rider for the first time since he'd gotten the man in his sights. "Is that so?"

"Yeah. I'll bet they've already sent someone else to come after us. They would have to be blind not to have seen us split away from the others and head over here. And with that being the case, I'd say they sent someone a little sneakier than those two to come after us while those others go after the cart and keep us distracted at the same time."

"And how are you so sure about this?"

Clint shrugged and replied, "It's what I would do."

That seemed to be good enough for Ned because he shook his head and turned his eyes back toward the approaching rider. The rider wasn't making a straight line for the cart but he was no longer angling directly for the trees, either.

"Looks like he won't be going around back of us," Ned said in a lower voice.

Clint was already up and headed toward the rear of the trees where Ned's horse and Eclipse were still tethered.

"Do what you can to discourage that one," he told Ned before he got too far away. "But try not to do anything too permanent. I'll take care of the one that's coming around this way."

"Or, you could stay here until you know for sure there's someone—" Ned stopped in mid-sentence and snapped his head up like a dog that had just heard a whistle. "Holy shit. You were right, Adams."

Clint had heard the other one coming as well. In fact, now that he'd been out in the elements for a while and he'd been straining his senses to their limits, he was no longer feeling so out of sorts. His eyes had adjusted to the glare, and his ears had heard enough of the background noise to be able to pick out which sounds didn't fit.

The sound of labored breathing and crunching dead leaves certainly didn't fit, especially when those noises were coming from a spot nowhere near the horses.

Up until then, Clint had been doing his best to keep one step ahead of the gang that was after them. His instincts had proven good enough to keep him ahead of the game just long enough for the rest of him to adjust to the cold.

Of course, now that he'd caught up, he had to keep himself alive.

TWENTY

The man came into the little wooded area on foot, having ditched his horse a few yards away so he could move quicker and quieter. His gang had spotted the glint of sunlight off of glass coming from those trees, and the man had been dispatched to rout out whoever had holed up there before they got wind of the others coming to take out the prisoner in the cart.

Not wanting to make any more noise than what was necessary, the man kept his hand on the grip of his pistol but did not draw. He was confident enough in his speed that he didn't plan on having any trouble outdrawing two men who would more than likely have their backs to him. Just thinking about that made the man smile.

Easy kills were always the best. Anyone who said any different was either bloodthirsty or still wet behind the ears. Professional assassins took a shot in the back over a gunfight anytime. Easy kills meant easy money and that was the name of the game.

They didn't get any easier than when the prey was sprawled out on the ground and looking in the other direction. The man tightened his grip on his pistol and took another step, making sure there was no way to miss once he drew and took his shot.

Suddenly, there came the sound of a single step followed by the rush of air. The next thing the man heard was the jarring crunch of his own nose being pounded into his skull and cartilage being turned into mush. It took a second for the pain to hit him, but when it did, it brought tears to his eyes and weakened him down to his knees.

Reflexively, the man drew his gun as he staggered back. The only problem was he didn't know exactly what he was shooting at. The target he'd spotted before was still lying in the same spot. As that thought raced through his mind, he saw a blur of motion coming from in front of him and to the left.

Clint stepped out from behind the tree he'd been leaning against and lifted the dead branch he'd picked up to use as a weapon. The branch had blood on it from the blow that had just been delivered to the other man's nose.

Just then, Clint heard the sound of gunshots in the distance. The sound came from the right direction and was far enough away to tell him that guns were being fired in the general vicinity of LeAnne and the cart. Those few shots were followed by the crackle of a few more. Clint didn't know which was worse: the sound of those shots or the chilling silence that followed.

He had more immediate concerns at the moment, however. Despite the blood and pain, the man on the ground was still making a grab for his gun. Clint had the upper hand, but he was also so close to the other fellow that only a miracle would prevent him getting hit if that rider pulled his trigger.

"Oh no you don't," Clint said as he snapped his wrists down and brought the branch into a short, straight chop.

The branch connected with the men's wrist before he could even attempt to fire. Because of Clint's speed and accuracy, the would-be ambusher dropped his gun without even getting off so much as a warning shot. Just to be certain, Clint swatted away the gun with a one-handed swing of the branch while using his other hand to pluck the modified Colt from its holster.

"You have any more weapons on you?" Clint asked.

Pressing the palms of his hands against his face to try to staunch the flow of blood coming from his nose, the other man spat out a few unintelligible curses. The mere effort of speaking was enough to send a fresh rush of pain through him, threatening to topple him into unconsciousness.

Ned walked up to Clint's side and watched the other man squirm on the ground. He chuckled a bit at the sight of the downed rider, who was flailing his legs while his upper body wobbled in an unsteady circle.

"What about that other one?" Clint asked.

"LeAnne took a few shots at him the moment he got close enough. He fired a few back but seemed to be more concerned with staying alive than with attacking that wagon on his own."

Clint saw the change in the the downed rider's eyes when he heard what Ned had said. Playing on that, Clint nodded and smirked down at the bleeding man.

"You hear that?" Clint asked. "Your partner out there was on his own."

"Vullshid," was the closest thing the other man could get to a curse with both hands clamped over a broken nose.

"If that was bullshit," Clint replied, "then how come there aren't more shots being fired? I don't even hear any of your partners shouting to each other. Isn't that odd?"

Over his blood-soaked hands, the fallen man's eyes darted back and forth as he waited to hear something to ease his worried mind. When he heard only the wind and the scraping of horses' hooves against the snow, the worry in him swelled to twice its original size.

"You see any more, Ned?"

After going back to check the lay of the land one more time, Ned returned with his report. "Nope. The wagon's rolling right along, and it looks like Sandra's already back with it. Hell, even them horses that were lined up are gone."

"What do you think, Ned? Should I kill him?"

"Sure. Why the hell not?"

Although the man with the broken nose hadn't said a word, the panic in his eyes spoke volumes. Clint was versed enough in reading faces to read each and every line of those volumes, as well as what lay between them.

After allowing a moment to go by, Clint stepped back and lowered his gun. "Actually, I think I'll let you get back to your masters and tell them what happened. But no matter what you tell them, be sure to remember two things.

"First of all, I don't like being ambushed. Second, this could have ended very differently for you here today. You and the rest of your gang should keep that in mind and ride on back into town, because if something like this happens again, we won't be so generous."

The man on the ground didn't say a word, but it was plain to see that he sure as hell got Clint's message.

TWENTY-ONE

The scout was still thinking about his run-in with Clint and Ned as he made his way back to where he knew Burt and the others were waiting. Several times along the way he considered not meeting up with the group, just picking any other direction to ride instead. He might have done it, too, if he still had a gun and wasn't shaky from the knocks he'd taken.

In the end, he decided to just face the music. He was too damn tired to do much of anything else. When he saw that there was nobody waiting in the spot where he'd left them, the scout's spirits actually took a turn for the better. If they were gone, then his decision was already made and he could just hobble into some other town for a fresh start.

That hope, no matter how feeble, was soon dashed. The others weren't exactly where they should have been, but they weren't that far away. He spotted Burt before any of the others—with his bulky frame and intense eyes, Burt could be seen through a blizzard. With those eyes focused on him, however, the scout knew there was a storm of a different kind headed his way. With that thought, the scout reverted to his original plan: it was time to face the music.

Burt was leading his horse by the reins and heading away from the rest of the group. The bulk of the gang was behind a cluster of rocks several yards from where they'd been lined up watching the cart's progress down the trail. Once he'd gotten around those rocks, the scout could see a few of the gang tending to the other scout as well as some members who were patching up more serious wounds.

"Where the hell have you been?" Burt asked in his brusque, accented voice.

"They headed me off."

"Who did?"

"Ned Gien and that other one."

"You mean Adams?"

The scout lowered his eyes, already anticipating Burt's reaction.

"Yeah."

"I told you to be careful, didn't I?" Burt exploded. Twisting around to look at the other scout laying on the ground closer to the rocks, he added, "I told both of you to watch yourselves. That you needed to step carefully around him and not try to prove anything just because of who he is."

Nodding toward his partner who was lying on the ground, the scout asked, "What happened to him?"

"His horse fell on top of him," Burt replied.

"What? Him and that horse have ridden through worse—"

"The horse didn't fall. It was tripped. Hobbled is more like it."

Hearing that, the scout looked around until he spotted the familiar animal. He rode over to the other man's horse, dropped from his saddle and bent to look at the animal's back legs. What caught his attention was the bandages that had been wrapped around the horse's ankles. Although some blood had soaked into the material and the horse was shifting uncomfortably on its feet, the wounds didn't keep it from standing.

Burt approached the animal as well, reaching out to pat it on the nose with a tenderness that didn't seem befitting a man with such cold eyes. "She'll be all right. The bitch that did this had a good touch with a blade. She even put these dressings on before leaving your friend over there for dead."

"A woman did this?" the scout asked.

"Don't act so surprised. A woman was also the one who did that," Burt said, pointing toward a pair of his other men who were tightening bandages around shoulder and leg wounds. "Wasn't the same woman, but that doesn't matter much."

"Are they shot?"

"When I didn't get a signal from either of you, I sent in someone to try for that cart. Since they didn't have any backup," Burt said while shooting a venomous glare at both of the scouts, "they pulled back before they got themselves shot up any worse."

"Like I said, they headed me off."

For a moment, the scout didn't know what to expect. He'd seen Burt deal with people who couldn't pull their weight and it was never pretty. It wasn't always fatal, but it sure as hell wasn't pretty.

Burt looked at the first scout who was stretched out on the ground and then turned his attention to the one standing beside him. "Looks like your nose is broke."

"It is, but I can manage."

"And did you at least get a good look at the men that did this to you?"

The scout nodded.

"And you won't let it happen again, will you?"

Feeling as though the clouds were lifting, the scout shook his head. "Not a chance in hell. They got lucky, is all."

Burt's hand lashed out in a blur of motion that was too quick for the scout to even see. His fist snapped outward and clipped the scout across the nose just hard enough to grind some of the shattered cartilage together. The resulting pain brought instant tears to the scout's eyes and a savage curse to his lips.

"Luck didn't have a damn thing to do with it," Burt snarled. "And if you can't recognize that, then I don't want you around."

In too much pain to string words together, the scout clamped his hands to his face and nodded as best he could. He saw Burt moving, and once he blinked away the fog inside his head, he noticed that Burt was actually moving away from him.

The men who'd been tending to the scout on the ground stepped aside when they saw the fire burning in their leader's eyes. The scout shifted and looked up at him but couldn't do much more than that.

"I think both his legs are broke," one of the men who'd been tending to the scout reported. "The horse was still on him when we found him."

"Can he walk?" Burt asked.

The other man shook his head despite the scout's insistence that he was feeling better. "One leg's busted for sure. The other's not doing too good."

"Can he ride?"

"Some of his ribs are cracked," the other said with a wince. "It'll be hard for a while, but—"

His words were cut off when Burt drew his pistol, pointed it and fired a round into the head of the scout below him. The scout's body seized up and then relaxed, spilling blood, brains and more into the soil beneath him.

At the sound of the gunshot, the entire gang stopped what they were doing and looked over to Burt. Although a few of them wore shocked expressions, none was a bit surprised. If anything, the other wounded among them moved their lips slightly in silent prayer that they wouldn't be the next ones in their leader's sights.

"We'll keep his horse," was all Burt said to fill the silence that fell upon the gang like a heavy blanket. "At least that one can do something besides hold us back."

Burt didn't say a word as he holstered his gun. The look in his eyes as he glanced at each of his men in turn was more than enough to get his point across. The look told each man that he needed to make himself useful or he would be cut away like so much dead weight.

When the remaining scout looked over at Frye, he saw the redhead smirking beneath his whiskers. "What's so damn funny?" he asked once Burt was safely away from them.

"I was just thinkin' about how much I'd hate to be riding with them folks and that cart out there. You think we've got it bad? God help Ned and those women once we catch up to 'em."

"And what about Adams?"

"Him?" Frye said with a shake of his head. "Not even God can do much to help him now."

TWENTY-TWO

Knowing that LeAnne and Mike had been shot at while he was among the trees, Clint found his imagination drifting inevitably toward the worst thoughts possible. It wasn't something he could help: those images just kept coming no matter how much he tried to hold them back. Being away from the rest of the group when there had been trouble made him second-guess his own decision to ride off with Ned.

Judging by the look on Ned's face, his thoughts weren't too far from Clint's. Once they'd dealt with the scout who'd come to ambush them, they quickly mounted up and rode to join LeAnne and Mike. At first they were unable to find either one. Then, after riding only a little ways down the trail they'd been using, they heard the familiar rattle of the cart's wheels on frozen ground.

Not only were LeAnne and Mike accounted for, but Sandra was with them as well. All three had their guns drawn and reflexively aimed them at Clint and Ned the moment they heard the sound of approaching horses.

"Take it easy," Clint said, reining Eclipse back so he didn't rush completely up to the others. "It's just me and Ned."

Sandra was the first to lower her weapon, acknowledging the other two with a nod. LeAnne followed suit and snapped her reins so she could rush up and greet the two men. Once she was within arm's reach, she leaned over and gave Clint a powerful hug. She even did the same for Ned, who appeared more surprised by the attention than by anything else that had happened that day.

"Jesus, I was worried about you," LeAnne said in a rush. "First Sandra disappeared, and then I didn't see hide nor hair of the two of you."

"We heard shots," Ned said, having just caught sight of some fresh bullet holes in the side of the cart. "Was anyone hurt?"

LeAnne shook her head. "They came at us, but we fought them off."

"They barely even got a shot off," Mike said, still keeping his rifle laying across his lap. "They barely even fought us before turning tail and running off."

Ned brought himself alongside the cart to get a closer look. Turning his eyes up toward the younger man, he said, "Don't get too full of yourself, kid. Those men were expecting to have numbers on their side but wound up with a little surprise of their own."

"I hit one of them," Mike said in his own defense. "I know it."

"Nobody's saying you didn't do good, kid. Just don't let your guard down while you're patting yourself on the back."

Although Mike had some more to say, he kept it to himself. Looking around, it was plain to see that nobody was thinking any less of him. The fact that he didn't get to go out away from the cart still grated on him, however. He wasn't even close to being able to hide that from anyone else in the group.

After returning LeAnne's hug as best he could while staying in his saddle, Clint looked over to Sandra, who rode by herself once again at the front of the line. The dark-haired woman's face was almost as cold as the land around her. It was hard to say whether she was hiding something or just trying to get herself back to normal, but one thing was certain. She had one of the best poker faces that Clint had ever come across.

TWENTY-THREE

Bringing Eclipse aside Sandra's mare, he rode quietly for a few seconds before asking, "What did you find out there?"

She shrugged. "Same thing you did, I'd expect. A few riders who thought they could pull one over on us."

"Did you run into any trouble?"

Laughing under her breath, she looked at him and said, "No, there wasn't any trouble at all. Just a gang trying to kill us and break this asshole out of our wagon. That's all."

"You know what I mean."

Sandra shifted her eyes away from Clint and set them on the same spot on the horizon that had held her attention earlier. "I found one and stopped him."

"Did you kill him?"

"No. I dropped his horse on top of him."

For a second, Clint thought she was kidding. But there was no mistaking the seriousness in her eyes. "How'd you manage that?"

She gave him a brief rundown of what had happened. By the end, she had a faraway, almost sad look in her eyes.

"You cut up a horse?" Ned asked, who'd been listening in from a few paces behind. "That's just wrong."

Ned's statement cut right to the essence of what had been bothering Sandra. "I cut up the rider's shirt and bandaged the horse's wounds the best I could. It was getting to its feet by the time I left, so just drop it."

"There's others out there, you know," came Mike's voice from the back of the group. "Shouldn't we be thinking about that? Or maybe we should be moving faster."

"He's got a point," Sandra said. "They may have pulled back for now, but I doubt they'll stay back for long."

Ned nodded grimly and looked at Clint. "From what I've heard about Burt, he's itching to throw some hell our way after the way we showed up his men. He don't make the same mistakes twice in a row."

"And neither do we," Clint said. He looked at each member of his group before settling his eyes on LeAnne. "You're the hunter here. What do you think Burt's next move might be?"

She thought about that for a second. Judging by the look on her face, Clint could tell that whatever was going through her mind wasn't pleasant. Eventually she said, "He's going to be mad as hell at what happened, but we've kept O'Connover from him a few times before and he never comes straight at us again right away."

"That's good, at least," Ned said.

"But when he does come back, it's from a different angle. Every time, he gets closer, and the only way we've stayed ahead of him this long is because we've been able to keep O'Connover locked up in a cell in the middle of town surrounded by gun hands."

"Gun hands?" Ned asked, beating Clint to the punch. "What gun hands are you talking about?"

"The ones that Bobby hired before any of you were approached for this job," LeAnne replied. "Burt cut through them after only two attacks to free O'Connover. That was what let us know just how serious this was." Turning to Clint, she added, "We've handled plenty of jobs like this, but we never got this much of a fight once we already had our man. Usually, there's a scuffle for a little while, but these guys keep coming like some kind of bad dream."

Ned shifted in his saddle and nodded as though Le-Anne had been talking to him the entire time. "Yeah," he mumbled, looking back at the site of the recent ambush. "One hell of a bad dream."

Although he didn't like someone constantly butting into his conversation, Clint could say little against Ned's sentiments. So far, Ned had been voicing what Clint and probably everyone else in the group was thinking. But LeAnne wasn't looking to Ned at the moment. She was looking to Clint and he wasn't about to leave her hanging.

"So how long does it usually take for Burt to pull his gang together and make another play for their man over there?" Clint asked.

This time, LeAnne didn't have to think for more than a fraction of a second. "A week or two at first. Lately, it's been less than that."

"And since we're out in the open, I'd say we should figure on him waiting for less than half that time now. Once men like that set their sights on what they want, they'll tear after it twice as fast. Have you ever gotten over on him this well before?"

That brought a smile to LeAnne's face. "Not even close. We managed to fight them back and maybe clip one or two of his boys here and there, but not like we did today."

"We bloodied that gang's nose pretty good," Clint agreed, without sharing LeAnne's enthusiasm. "But that only means the leader will take a more personal stake in things. He must know we're at our weakest point out here in the open, so there's no reason for him to hold back."

"Well, you've proved yourself to me, Adams," Ned said. "I'm willing to give you the benefit of the doubt here. So, with all due respect, what are we supposed to do now besides just wait to get hit again, knowing it's gonna be worse the next time around?"

"We do what we've all been paid to do," Clint replied. "This is all over as soon as O'Connover gets where he needs to go. I was hired on to lend a hand with transport, not to wipe out this gang. Once we finish our job, the other problem should resolve itself. That leaves only the original task that brought us all here."

LeAnne smiled at Clint as she said, "That's why Bobby wanted you with us so bad. You keep things moving in the right direction."

"Yeah, well, don't get too happy just yet," Sandra said while looking over her shoulder from the head of the line. "We may have some other problems to contend with besides that gang."

"What are you talking about?" Clint asked.

She pointed ahead at a mass of clouds so thick that it resembled a gray wall in the sky. "Storm's coming. Could be a big one."

Clint's mind took that in and put it together with everything else.

"We should be able to get around the worst of it and add only a few more days to our ride," Sandra pointed out.

"I've got a better idea," Clint said. "Let's go right through the middle of it."

"What?" LeAnne and Ned asked in unison.

Clint's eyes were already set on those clouds as well as the path that led right beneath them. "They'd be crazy to follow us, wouldn't they?"

TWENTY-FOUR

To the casual eye, the clouds might not have looked too much different than those that sullied any winter day. They'd rolled in from the north, creeping along at a slow enough pace to dim the sun's light gradually rather than blacking it out altogether. Over the rest of the day, the clouds grew more ominous, hanging like ragged shrouds above their heads. Sandra was no casual observer, however, and her face became increasingly worried as more of the sunlight was blotted out.

It was late in the day and the group had been riding at an even quicker pace than they had earlier. The air grew colder with each passing hour, and the wind took on a more steely edge as it tore through the barren trees and raked over the snow-covered ground. That wind, the rumble of the cart's wheels and the fall of hooves were the only sounds the group could hear.

It was a stark contrast to the gunfire and shouting that had filled everyone's ears earlier, but it was a welcome contrast. Once everyone had found their rhythm, they settled in and focused on the trail ahead. Although it hadn't been officially stated, Clint became the leader of the group simply because he'd been the one to step up and take

control. He was pretty certain that Bobby had planned it
that way and was glad he hadn't been forced on everyone
as the man in charge.

With personalities as strong as the ones along for this
ride, things had to be handled the right way to avoid as
much friction as possible. So far, Clint couldn't have been
happier with the people in the group. Each one had their
strengths, and even Mike was proving to be a valuable
asset because he was willing to put himself behind whatever needed doing.

Sandra remained at the head of the group. Her eyes
were sharper than a hawk's, and she seemed to navigate
using finely honed instinct as much as her other senses.
Ned brought up the rear. That was their most vulnerable
spot, and he had the nose of a hunter, which meant he
could sniff out a threat coming long before it got there.

Mike drove the cart, which freed up Clint and LeAnne
to drift among the group as they went along. When they
came to a spot of rough road, Clint would scout ahead to
prepare the way. Similarly, LeAnne would scout ahead
whenever terrain or cloud cover obscured their view.

LeAnne moved with swift confidence and was more
familiar with the land than Clint. When she needed to
make a scouting run, she would touch the spurs to her
horse and be off like a shot. She returned each time with
a change in course already planned to keep them on track.

Everyone in the group was wise enough to be troubled
by what lay ahead of them: they were headed straight into
the gaping maw of a storm just about to break. As they
got closer and the day started to fade into night, they felt
the storm's presence circling them like a hungry wolf.

Clint was no stranger to hard rides. He'd made his way
through terrain of all sorts ranging from swamps to de-
serts, and each of them carried its own set of dangers.
Any number of those dangers could be fatal, and the tricks
of the cold were no exception.

In the cold, falling asleep at the wrong time could be the last mistake a man ever made. And because this time he was responsible not only for himself but others as well, Clint was particularly glad to have the help of experts. Their aid would make the trip go smoother, and once darkness fell on that first day, he was more than pleased with Bobby's choices.

They rode as much into the night as they could, stopping only when Sandra said it was absolutely necessary. They had gathered wood along the way, so building a fire took hardly any time at all. Considering they still had a gang of killers dogging their tail, they kept the fire small. The entire group huddled around the little crackling flames, the warmth a godsend to frozen hands.

They slept in shifts. While three slept a few hours, the other two stood watch and tended to the fire. They kept the flames alive, but just barely. The camp itself was only slightly warmer than the unforgiving land around them.

They woke the next day before the sun came up and were moving by dawn. Although their spirits seemed high, they talked little about the end of their ride. They still had too much ground to cover to think about that.

The trial north stretched out like the bumpy spine of a dead, frozen animal, and there was no end in sight.

TWENTY-FIVE

When the sun crested over the hills to the east, Clint was able to handle the light much better than he had the day before. He was no longer blinded by the glare, and he noticed that his ears were getting even better at picking out subtle sounds over the constant roar of the wind.

"You look a little better today," LeAnne said, bringing her horse up next to Eclipse.

Clint laughed and said, "I didn't know I looked so terrible before."

"Not terrible, just a little more run down. It looks to me like you're getting used to the cold."

"I was used to it before. Hell, I've ridden through worse."

"Riding is one thing. Keeping sharp and being as alert as you'd be in the warmer months is something else. The cold does something to you that you can never really prepare for. Things seem brighter and pain sticks with you longer."

"Well, I have noticed that I don't have to squint so much today as I did yesterday."

"There you go. It's like folks who live in the desert.

They don't mind the heat or the sand in their boots as much as others."

"It's nice to know that I'm not just getting frail in my old age," Clint chided. "But it's going to be a long time before I get used to the feel of snow in my boots."

"Just give it time," Ned said from the back of the group. "By the end of this ride, you'll be ready to strip down and run through a drift just to get your eyes open in the morning."

Clint twisted around to get a look at the other man and saw that Ned wasn't completely kidding. The proof of that was in the easy way he rode through the blustery winds with his coat hanging open as though he was enjoying a cool autumn day. Ned's skin was a dark red that came from the frigid temperature instead of the sun.

"I said I was getting better," Clint replied. "Not that I was going crazy."

Ned flashed a smile and winked. "Give it time, Adams. Stay out in this cold long enough and it'll get to you. Whether you feel it anymore or not, it'll get to you."

Although she surely heard everything everyone said, Sandra chose to ignore what came out of Ned's mouth more often than not. "You know what helps?" she offered. "Think about your toes."

"Your toes?" Ned asked as if he'd just been told to sprout horns.

Clint didn't exactly understand where she was headed yet either, but he could see the look on her face. She gazed ahead as though she was looking at a garden oasis. Her eyes were relaxed and a gentle smile had come across her face.

"Just think about your toes," Sandra said. "Right now. Wiggle them in your boots and feel every one of them."

As stupid as it sounded, everyone in the group did as she suggested. They all went quiet as they concentrated and wiggled their toes. At any other time, they might have laughed at the notion. But with nothing around them except snowy woods and their destination nowhere in sight, thinking about toes was at least something to pass the time.

"Now think about how warm they are," Sandra continued. "The more you wiggle them, the more they move in your boots and in your socks, the warmer they get."

After a few more quiet moments, Ned broke the silence.

"Aw, this is—"

"Just shut up and think, Ned," Sandra interrupted. "I know it may hurt you to think, but do it for me."

Grumbling, he shut his eyes and said, "All right, but you owe me."

She ignored him and let her smile come back before going on. "Now take that warmth and feel it run up through your legs. Think of warming yourself by a fire or pulling a blanket over yourself from the bottom up. Spread that warmth all the way up until you think about that blanket wrapping you from top to bottom. Think about the sun or the summer or whatever is the warmest thing you can think of and spread it around until you feel it all over your body."

As she finished talking, Sandra closed her eyes as well. The entire group seemed lost in thought for the next minute or so until finally Ned broke the little spell that had fallen over them.

"I'll be damned," he said.

Clint snapped his eyes wide open, suddenly realizing that he'd let himself drift off for a moment. "That's a good trick," he said. "Up to a few minutes ago, I couldn't even feel my toes."

LeAnne nodded. "Only problem with getting so comfortable is having to start moving again. But I've got to hand it to you, Sandra. I feel like I just rolled out of bed. What about you, Mikey?" she asked, twisting around to look at the younger man driving the cart. "You feel any warmer?"

Mike didn't say anything at first, but when he did, his voice sounded like rusty hinges grating together. "I guess. But all the warm thinking in the world won't help me until I can pry my ass off this goddamn seat."

As always, Ned was the first one to react to what had been said, laughing so hard that he wound up bent forward in his saddle. The rest of the group joined in with laughter of their own until everyone was practically out of breath. After all that had happened to get them where they were, it felt good to let go and have a good laugh, and everyone savored the moment for all it was worth.

Clint was catching his breath when he heard something that brought him back to the here and now. It was the sound of muffled laughter coming from inside the cart, and it reminded him of precisely why they were traveling in the middle of a frozen woodland.

"Where are you going?" LeAnne asked when she saw Clint break from his position toward the front and move closer to the wagon.

"I think I'll give Ned a change of scenery and switch places with him for a while."

Before she could say anything else, LeAnne saw Ned racing toward her and gladly taking up position beside her.

TWENTY-SIX

Only two other men rode with Burt while he skirted along the edge of a low ridge. The rest of the gang was scattered within a mile of each other, each smaller group taking a slightly different path, but all heading in the same direction.

Every one of the gang members had the same purpose in mind: to watch Clint and the others like hawks and pick the perfect moment to strike. With the smell of blood still fresh in their noses and the sound of gunfire still ringing in their ears, they knew they'd damn well better do their jobs.

It was either that or wind up dead and half buried in the snow like the man they'd left behind.

Burt felt the cold slice through him but didn't do a thing to keep himself warm. He didn't button one more button or even turn his collar up to keep the winter's breath from freezing his neck. He embraced the cold. As the temperature fell even lower and the skies became an even more steely shade of gray, Burt simply gritted his teeth and forced himself through it.

"We shouldn't be following them into that storm," Frye said in a vaguely trembling manner as he rode at

Burt's side. Until now, no matter how much he'd been thinking it, Frye had kept himself from actually saying those words. But when it became obvious that they were going to ride straight into hell, Frye knew he had to say something.

Burt smirked and let out a gruff laugh. "I was wondering who would be the first one to say that."

"I figured I don't have anything to lose. You may shoot me, but if we keep going we may all freeze to death in there anyhow. Dead is dead, Burt. Except if we keep going, it may be every last one of us that disappears until the spring thaw."

Pulling in a deep breath, Burt held it inside his lungs and felt the cold nip at his innards like a school of hungry piranha. "If I had any doubt that that man up there was Clint Adams, it got burned away with that botched raid we tried yesterday."

Frye narrowed his eyes, unsure if Burt had even really heard what he'd said. "Yeah?"

"You know the difference between a man with real strength and a man who just flaps his gums?"

Frye was confused. He thought he'd stepped far enough out of line that he would at least be tasting Burt's knuckles by now. Instead, the conversation had taken a turn with no threatening consequences in sight. Then again, not many had seen it coming when Burt had killed his scout the day before, either.

Looking over at Frye and recognizing the baffled expression on his face, Burt went on with what he was saying.

"Strength is doing what nobody else has the guts to do, even if it's just to prove a point," Burt said. "It's stepping up and facing down someone or something twice your size and coming out on top without having to bat an eye. That's strength.

"Clint Adams has that strength, Frye. I've seen it before and I saw it again yesterday. He's riding into that storm because it's the best way to put some space between us and him." Burt took a breath, and then his tone shifted from conversational to deadly serious.

"And while he's showing me his strength, my own men do nothing but show they got nothing between their goddamn legs once it's time to stop flapping gums and start stepping up. So you think we shouldn't go into that storm, huh?"

Burt's tone sent a chill through Frye much colder than the chill from the air. "I think we need to think this through before we just follow. We take a wrong step out here, and there ain't no coming home."

Burt took another breath, held it and let the steam seep out from behind clenched teeth. "You feel that? You feel that cold go through you like a saw blade?"

That alone was enough to make every muscle in Frye's body twitch. "Yeah, and I've been feeling it ever since that first snow."

"You need to look at things like this cold, that storm and Clint Adams as a way to test your own strength. The strong like Adams go into the breech when the time's right, and they walk out. Well, we're headed into that damn storm, Frye, and them that don't come home were too damn weak to live anyhow."

"But it's suicide, Burt. Strong or not, we don't put a gun to our head and pull the trigger."

"Maybe you don't," Burt said, placing his hand over the grip of his pistol. "But if I see a man weak enough to slow us down, I will put my gun to his head and pull the trigger. Think back and you'll remember that I'm telling the truth on that count."

Frye didn't have to think back. Once he heard Burt's voice drop to that certain pitch, he knew damn well what was about to be said. After that he waited to feel the touch of cold steel against his temple before the lead was blasted through his skull.

But the shot didn't come.

"We'll make it through this storm," Burt said.

To Frye, those words came like the voice of the Almighty. He was that surprised to be alive.

"That storm's nothing but wind and snow and ice," Burt continued. "Storms come and go and plenty of people see them through. You know why we'll make it through? Because I'll pull every last one of you through it myself if I have to. I need all the help I can get to get through Adams. Besides, did you forget why we're doing this?"

Blinking as though he'd caught a splash of water in his eyes, Frye shook his head. "No. I haven't."

"O'Connover's still out there and we're the only thing standing between him and Canada. You know what happens if he makes it to the law that's waiting for him over the border?"

"Yeah."

"Then why the hell are you worried about some goddamn storm?"

A few moments before, Frye was certain he was going to die by Burt's hand. Now, he set his jaw in a grim line, shut his mouth and rode right into the churning mass of icy death that was rolling down from the north.

TWENTY-SEVEN

It felt later than it was, mainly because the clouds were billowing down to swallow up the sun before it had a chance to set. Despite the laughter they'd shared and the easy companionship that followed, the members of Clint's party had once again drifted into their own little worlds. It wasn't unusual. It was what happened when a person spent so many hours sitting in a saddle and watching the world flow beneath his dangling feet.

Clint had taken his position at the back of the line next to the cart and stayed there. One reason for that was to keep his senses sharp. The other reason was to become a fixture outside the cart and thereby forgotten by the man inside of it.

Although he'd succeeded in one of those tasks, Clint knew for certain that the other had no chance. Every part of him had acclimated to the cold in ways that Clint never thought possible. He'd either gotten used to it, ignored it or just forced himself to fight through it. He felt much less vulnerable than when his teeth had still been chattering.

Those acclimated senses told him that the man inside the cart was watching him just as much as he was being watched. The sounds of movement inside of that cramped box were few and far between. When Clint got the occasional glimpse into the cart thanks to a stray ray of light, he saw a pair of eyes staring right back out at him.

"Hello in there," Clint said with a nod toward the cart. Although he didn't get an answer, Clint saw O'Connover's face shift and his eyes narrow.

"You warm enough?"

O'Connover's humorless laugh sounded like heavy furniture scraping against a wooden floor. "You're worried about my health?"

"I'm no undertaker," Clint said. "I'm not in the habit of carting around dead bodies. You need anything, you let me know."

"Wanna keep your cargo alive, huh? That's real touching."

"That cart took a couple bullets yesterday. I figured if you were hurt, you'd let us know. Now I'm not so sure."

"I die in here or I die out there," O'Connover grumbled. "Makes no difference to me."

Sensing the resolve in O'Connover's voice, Clint made sure the other man could see him shrug through the little opening in the rear door of the cart. "Suit yourself," he said before flicking Eclipse's reins and moving back into his spot a little farther from the cart.

O'Connover watched from the shadows. The thin wisps of his breath curled from his nostrils and drifted in front of him as the cart rumbled onward.

It was getting close to dark when the party came to a stop. Sandra signaled for the halt with an upraised hand. Having become accustomed to her gestures, everyone else obeyed the request immediately and headed for the spot that she led them to so they could all stretch their legs.

Clint waited for Mike to climb down from the driver's seat and walk away from the cart before heading around

back of the wooden box on wheels. Leaning down so he
could look straight into the cart, he checked to make sure
that O'Connover was still awake and not frozen into a
ball.

"When was the last time you were out of there?" Clint
asked.

"What do you care?"

Shrugging, Clint didn't say another word before turning and stepping away from the cart.

"It's been a while," came a voice from inside the four
wooden walls.

Clint stopped, turned around and walked back to the
cart. This time, when he looked in, he put his face up
close to the opening so he could see more than just the
other man's eyes. O'Connover sat huddled in the cart surrounded by other solid shapes covered in burlap. The prisoner's limbs were wrapped tightly around him just as
Clint had expected. There just wasn't any other way for
a grown man to fit into that space.

"Move back," Clint ordered.

"Make this cart bigger and I'll give it a shot."

When Clint spoke again, his voice was a low, delib-
erate rumble that delivered its intention with deadly accuracy. "Move . . . back."

Letting out an aggravated breath, O'Connover placed
his feet against the back wall and shuffled as far back as
he could. He pressed his shoulders against the front wall
of the cart and even positioned himself so his body was
jammed against the dark shapes surrounding him.

Holding his head cocked at an awkward angle against
the cart's roof, O'Connover said, "This better?"

"Much," Clint replied. Only then did he dig in his
pocket for the keys to the lock that held the cart shut.

The moment she heard the sound of metal on metal,
LeAnne rushed back to see why the key was turning inside that lock. "What are you doing, Clint?" she asked.

"Checking on our passenger."

"First off, he's not a passenger. He's a prisoner. And if you want to give him a chance to get away from us, then go ahead and let him out of there."

"The man needs to get some sun on his face before it goes down for another day. Or were you just planning on throwing him bread crumbs while we dragged him through the snow like a human plow?"

LeAnne stared at Clint for a few seconds and when she saw that he wasn't budging, she threw up her hands. "Fine. But if anything happens, it's your fault."

"Nice to know you've got me covered," Clint said before turning the key. When he opened the door and looked inside, he said, "Wipe that smirk off your face, O'Connover, before I take the lady's advice."

TWENTY-EIGHT

Watching O'Connover emerge from the cart, Clint wondered what LeAnne was so worried about in the first place. Not only was the prisoner's every movement hindered by the pain of being cooped up, but he was also wrapped in more steel than the driver of a locomotive.

Chains rattled like hail on a tin roof as O'Connover scooted out from the back of the cart. Chains connected the shackles on his ankles, more chains connected the cuffs around his wrists and all the chains were locked together by yet another chain wrapped around his waist.

O'Connover dangled his legs off the edge of the cart and took a long breath of air that hadn't been filtered through the wooden walls of his portable cell. For a moment, Clint thought the other man was just savoring his first taste of the outside. Then O'Connover looked up at him and leaned forward.

"You missed one," he said, showing Clint the chain that was locked to a steel ring at the back of the cart.

Clint was fairly certain the prisoner was in no condition to run but took all precautions anyhow as he unlocked the final lock inside the cart. O'Connover waited right where Clint had put him until that last chain loosened its grip.

"Come on," Clint said as he pocketed the keys. "Let's take a little walk."

O'Connover shuffled a few noisy steps before stopping and holding out his cuffed hands. "Think you could loosen these a bit? It feels like my hands and feet are about to come off."

"Then walk real carefully."

"Just for a little w—"

"Don't push your luck, O'Connover. You want to walk or do you want to waste your time trying to sweet-talk me?"

O'Connover shuffled forward without another word. The chains dangled from him and dragged behind as well, leaving a deep trail in the snow.

Clint didn't take him far. Everyone else was watching him, but LeAnne was keeping them back. All of those intense stares gave Clint a taste of what it must feel like to be on stage. Either that, or maybe at the receiving end of a firing squad.

"I thought everyone had forgotten about me in there," O'Connover said.

"Not hardly. Without you in there, we'd all be in front of a nice, warm fire somewhere. We'd sure be eating better, that's for certain."

"Whatever you're eating can't compare to the stale bread and jerky that gets tossed in at me."

Clint looked over at O'Connover and found the same thing coming to mind that had been nagging at him since the first time he'd visited him in the jailhouse. "You don't act much like an outlaw," Clint said.

"What should I be doing? Screaming and spitting at you?"

"Not exactly." He couldn't even put his finger on what it was. Something about O'Connover just didn't set right. "You never told me what you did to wind up in that cell.

Or what could have gotten the Canadian law so riled up that they want you so badly."

As always, O'Connover shrugged rather than answer the question. "It don't matter anymore, does it? I'm here and soon I'll be there. End of story."

"Maybe it's the end, but it'd make a whole lot more sense to me if I heard the entire story first."

O'Connover looked at Clint, studying him. His eyes took on a sharpness that seemed to see down to the bottom of Clint's soul. Plenty of prisoners got that look in their eyes, but usually it took years of being locked away for them to develop it. After all, when all a man could do was watch, he usually got real good at it.

"Do you really want to hear what I got to say?" O'Connover asked. "Or are you just lookin' to find out what I know?"

"That's an odd question. What is it that you know?"

Cocking his head slightly, O'Connover asked, "You really don't know, do you?"

"Jesus, O'Connover, just spit it out. I'm listening."

Shifting his eyes quickly to spot where the others were standing, the prisoner leaned a little closer to Clint and whispered, "Those others that're after me. They're not trying to break me out. They're trying to kill me."

Dozens of questions flooded Clint's mind. He didn't get a chance to ask a single one of them, however, before Sandra's voice sounded out.

"We gotta move," she shouted. "And I mean right now."

Clint could feel the storm bearing down on them. This time, though, he knew the snow and wind weren't the only things waiting to drop on top of them.

TWENTY-NINE

Hearing O'Connover's statement put a lot of things into perspective for Clint. It also answered many of the questions that he'd been pondering during the empty hours spent riding over the frozen trail.

For one thing, it explained why O'Connover wasn't acting as most men in his position would act. He hadn't made any real attempts to break out or even resist when he'd been transported from one cell to another. He seemed resigned to his fate and none too excited when Burt and the rest of his gang made an attack on Clint, LeAnne or the rest.

But what counted for more in Clint's mind was that certain intangible factor that came into play so much in his life. Not only did O'Connover's words make sense, but they also felt right. His statement wasn't enough to stand up in a court of law or even to convince anyone else in the party, but it was enough for Clint.

Weather permitting, the group figured on making it into Canada after another day or two. Then again, everyone felt pretty lucky that the weather had permitted them to travel as far as they had in just two days' time.

The snow was already falling in fluffy waves, and the

temperature had dropped noticeably in the space of a few hours. Just as Clint prepared himself to cover the last couple miles of the day, he was stopped by the sight of Sandra's raised hand.

"We'll camp here tonight," she said.

Clint rode up to where she'd stopped as everyone else halted and started climbing down from their saddles. "We can make it a bit farther before the light's gone," he said.

"We could, but we won't find a better spot than this to camp."

"Are you sure about that?"

"Yes," she said without hesitation. "I am."

Nodding, Clint tried not to sound as if he was giving orders when he said, "All right, I'll give you that one. But we're trying to go as far as we can as quickly as we can. If we need to sacrifice a better campsite for the sake of covering more ground, then that's what we should do."

Sandra looked around and saw that all the others had stopped what they were doing so they could watch the exchange between herself and Clint. Lowering her voice and bringing her horse up a little closer to Eclipse, she said, "I know Bobby hired you to make tough calls, but he hired me because I know what I'm doing when it comes to making it through what's coming. Sure, we could push on a little more, but we might not be able to get moving as quickly tomorrow. You see the way the ground slopes down from where we're standing?"

Clint looked at where she was pointing and nodded. "Yeah."

"And you feel the snow that's hitting your face right now?"

Already, Clint could tell that more of the snow was sticking to him as well as to the ground than had been earlier. This time, he could feel the weight of the snow on his shoulders, and what little of it that melted against his body heat quickly became ice when the wind blew over him.

"There's going to be plenty more snow where that came from," Sandra continued. "It'll blow down that ridge rather than collect here. Also, rolling that cart downward will give us a running start tomorrow morning. Without that, we may waste half the day trying to dig out and drag that damn cart uphill."

Even as he listened to her, Clint knew Sandra was right. Not only that, he also realized just how entrenched he'd been within his desire to keep moving and get everyone north of the border. Holding up his hands in surrender, Clint said, "I surrender. You win."

"I didn't mean to make this into a fight, but—"

"You weren't," Clint interrupted. "I was doing that just fine on my own. I needed someone to lift my eyes from the trail ten feet in front of me so I could see the big picture."

Sandra looked as though she wasn't sure if Clint was truly admitting he'd been wrong. Finally she said, "I usually don't hear that I'm right. At least not from men like you."

"And exactly what kind of man am I?"

"I don't know," she answered with a wry grin. "But I wouldn't mind finding out."

They took a moment to relax from the tension that had built up between them. Everyone else must have sensed the change as well because they were going back to doing what they'd been doing before.

"I need to get some extra provisions," Sandra said. "And some wood for a fire."

"We can do that," Clint said. "Why don't you take a rest for a bit? I'll take first watch."

"I need them because I need to scout ahead."

"What? Tonight?"

She nodded. "I have to see how bad the storm's hit the

trail in front of us. We may need to take a different road if one's too buried to use. Also, I need to see if Burt's been able to get ahead of us. If we run into another ambush on top of that storm, we'll be biting off more than anyone can chew."

Clint shook his head. He felt his pulse quickening again, but this time it wasn't out of frustration. "No. We need to stick together."

"I'm the scout here, remember? Let me do my job."

"And my job is to make sure we don't get killed along the way."

"Unless you haven't been paying attention, that's everyone's job." Sandra took a deep breath and let it out. "Look, I need to scout ahead, and if I don't go now, I'll only go later."

"Then I'll go with you. You know you shouldn't go far on your own at night, in a storm and with a gang sneaking up on us."

"And you shouldn't go far from the main thing that the gang's after."

Each of them had good points and the other one knew it. Of course, that put them both at something of a loss.

"I'll go along," Ned said from where he'd been listening in. "Clint, you and the rest can stay here and I'll go with Sandra. I'm probably the only one that can move as quickly and quietly as she can. With both of us on the job, we'll be back before you know it."

"All right, then," Sandra said before Clint could get a word in. "That's settled."

Even if Clint wanted to argue, he didn't have a chance to string three words together before Sandra and Ned charged off.

THIRTY

The storm hit them like the proverbial ton of bricks.

It came as soon as darkness fell, like a giant predator that had been waiting for the best time to strike. Clint and Mike had just gone out to gather more firewood when the wind shifted from a gusting howl to a full-throated roar. The wind was fearsome enough on its own, but the snow and bits of ice it carried provided the bite to go along with the powerful bark.

The members of the group were used to keeping track of time by watching the sun pass overhead. But when that storm rolled upon them, it stole away the last precious minutes of light, enveloping them in cold, pitch black.

When they returned, Clint and Mike found LeAnne already coaxing a campfire to life. She had gotten the flames going, but not by much. With the storm howling, she was lucky to keep more than a spark alive. As they moved around the camp, no one bothered to say a word. Time was too short for talk, and they each knew their tasks well enough anyway. LeAnne worked at the fire, slowly adding more wood, while Clint and Mike rushed around setting up two of the small tents they carried in their supplies.

All the while, O'Connover sat huddled in his wooden cell. The irony of it was that he was more comfortable in captivity than any of his captors were out in the open. Clint looked in on him once, but O'Connover signaled that he was doing fine wrapped up in two of the blankets that had been stored there with the other supplies.

The sun had set by the time the camp was prepared. Every inch of ground as well as every leaf and branch on every tree was already covered with snow. That blanket of white reflected the light from the stars and moon until the whole world took on a dull glow.

Clint and Mike settled down next to the fire. LeAnne was huddled there, watching the crackling flames and waiting to pounce at the first sign of the fire dying out. They sat there, still not saying a word to one another. This time, they were just too tired to speak.

As they rubbed their hands together, trying to soak up what little heat the fire offered, they could feel the storm sinking its teeth deeper and deeper into them. The snow was getting thicker. The wind was picking up, and while it already felt impossibly cold, it was somehow getting colder.

"Jesus," Mike sputtered. "I've never felt this cold before." His words came out in a rush as though he knew they'd only freeze in his throat if he didn't push them out quickly.

Clint lifted his eyes to the sky. The cloud cover was almost complete, but through a few patches that looked like rips torn in fabric, he could see the stars and the moon. Those patches of sky gave the night its glow but did nothing to lessen the snow that continued to dump on them.

"We're in it now, all right," Clint said. "I can't say for sure, but it doesn't look like the end's anywhere in sight."

LeAnne shook her head. "Those clouds are moving slow. Otherwise we would've been in this much sooner."

"That would've been better, I think," Mike said. "At least that way we would've been out of it that much faster."

Clint got up and went to fetch the pots and pans to cook dinner. He cooked beans and thick cuts of bacon. Mike made the coffee while LeAnne continued to keep a close eye on the fire. Getting the food truly hot would have taken forever, so Clint settled for slightly warm before dishing it out to the other two.

They ate quickly, devouring their food before the storm could turn it stone cold on their plates. The coffee, despite its lukewarm temperature, felt like a taste of heaven when it trickled down their throats.

When dinner was over, Clint went back to the cart to put the supplies away. "Here," he said, tossing in the supplies next to O'Connover. "And here's something I set aside for you."

O'Connover took the food that Clint handed him and wolfed it down immediately. "You wouldn't have any coffee for me, would you?"

Clint handed over a cup half full of the warm drink. Standing there, he recalled what O'Connover had said to him the last time they had talked. Although he wanted to continue that discussion, Clint knew there was a proper time and place for everything. Hearing the prisoner's side of things was important, but making it through the night was even more so.

Already the cart's wheels were becoming lost in the drifting snow. The horses needed to be wrapped in blankets, and the cart had to be kept somewhat clear or their job the next morning would be that much bigger. Satisfied that O'Connover was as safe as he could be under the circumstances, Clint closed up the cart and began working on the other tasks that needed to be done.

The cold affected a man in a strange way. As it seeped into a body, it acted like a slow watchman snuffing out

candles one at a time. Rather than candles, this watchman
dimmed the fire inside a person's blood. The colder the
blood, the slower the person moved. The slower he
moved, the more tired he became until all he wanted was
to lie down and go to sleep.

Anyone with the least bit of experience knew that giving into that kind of sleep meant never waking up again.
A person that cold was only inches away from freezing.

It was not the time to talk.

It was not the time to sit idle.

Clint, LeAnne and Mike had jobs to do. It was a time
for them to show why they'd been chosen to go on this
job.

But more important, it was a time for each member of
the party to keep the others alive.

THIRTY-ONE

Sandra rode as if her horse's tail were on fire. She bolted through the low hanging branches and jumped over the roots that had busted up from the ground as though none of those obstacles were even there. She'd chosen her horse for this ride not only because of its ability to blend in with its environment, but also because it had a special talent for keeping its balance no matter what.

Riding a few paces behind her, Ned had plenty of time to admire the animal's fine lines and graceful form as it charged onward off the beaten trail. Snow churned as they passed, creating their own trail as they went. For any other riders, riding so fast over such uncertain ground might have been a problem. But they weren't just any riders.

Of course, that didn't mean that it was easy to ride over rugged terrain covered by newly fallen snow. The riders felt every step the animals took. Sandra and Ned concentrated on every fall of the hooves as well as every shift of their horses' bodies. Ned could tell by the way she was riding that Sandra was trying to lose him in the dark. But the longer they rode, the more their eyes became accustomed to the luminescent glow of the snowy night.

And the more he adjusted, the more Ned could allow himself to enjoy what he was seeing.

Chasing Sandra was like following a wildcat as it bounded and raced through its territory. Her body moved perfectly in tune with her horse, and although she remained firmly on her saddle, her form was in constant motion. Her hips shifted as the horse went through the occasional skid, and her legs tightened or loosened their grip when necessary to either hang on or let the animal move more freely. Ned didn't have too much trouble keeping up, but it took everything he had to do so. Sandra, on the other hand, appeared to be just getting started.

When she looked over her shoulder, she seemed more than a little surprised to see him tailing her so well. A little smile even appeared on her face as she turned her eyes back onto the trail ahead. After breaking through a stand of trees, she pulled back on the reins just enough to slow down her horse. Ned did the same, and after allowing some of their momentum to fade, they both finally came to a stop.

Ned brought his horse up close to her, looking over so he could get a lingering view of her face. Sandra's mouth was parted slightly, which was a beautiful sight in itself. Her upper lip was a thin red line while the lower one was plump and soft even in the bitter elements. In fact, her skin seemed to be holding up just fine in the cold. More than that, it suited her.

Wisps of steam drifted from between those lips as she let her breath flow in and out. Her cheeks were flushed after the vigorous ride and her hands were wrapped around the reins with a gentle strength that made certain she would never let them go.

"You see them?" she asked in a velvety whisper.

It was an effort for Ned to take his eyes off her face and turn them toward the point in the distance at which Sandra was staring. Squinting to focus in the odd blend of pale light and utter dark, Ned quickly picked out two shapes less than a quarter of a mile away.

"Yeah," he said. "I see 'em both. You think they followed us?"

Sandra shook her head. "If I only just spotted them a few seconds ago, there's no way they could have been watching us for much longer. Not through this storm, anyway."

Ned turned his face toward the sky. In the heat of the chase and all the thoughts that followed, the storm had been the last thing on his mind. Now that he wasn't so distracted, he could feel the pelting of ice and snow against his head and shoulders. The back of his throat felt so cold that it was about to crack, but he knew better than to do something so foolish as to swallow as he wanted to.

Bringing his hand up to his lips, Ned tipped his wrist to dump a portion of snow into his mouth. The snow melted and he tipped his head back to allow the moisture to run over his throat before swallowing and working the muscles back there.

"You think there's any more of them around?" he asked, forcing himself to turn away from the oncoming wind.

"There's more out there, you can be sure of that. The only question is if there's any more of them closer to where the others are camped."

"You don't think we have to worry about them?" Ned asked, nodding toward the figures cowering beneath the wind in the distance.

Sandra let out a short laugh that came out as a puff of steam from her mouth. "Those two? They're not going anywhere anytime soon. If they were, they wouldn't be sitting still for so long."

"Well, maybe they've just never dealt with a storm like this one." Lifting his nose to the wind, Ned added, "And it feels like it's gonna get a whole lot worse before it gets better."

"Yeah, and if those two don't know what they're doing, then we won't have to worry about them. They'll be frozen solid before sunrise."

Ned nodded at the cold finality of Sandra's words. There was no emotion in her statement, just plain facts. Some folks might have been put off by the way she regarded death as just another possible outcome. Ned wasn't one of those folks. In fact, he was quite the opposite.

"You think they see us?" he asked.

Sandra looked over at him and fixed her eyes on his. "Do I really need to answer that?"

Ned glanced over at the two figures. He could see little more than outlines, but he could tell that the riders hadn't spotted them. Their movements were too random and their horses kept shifting too far as they paced back and forth. The riders were restless and most likely trying to figure out what they should do or where they should go next.

Sandra was right. They wouldn't make it through the night.

"Those poor bastards," Ned hissed.

Sandra's reply was unconvincing. "Yeah. It's a real shame. Come on, we've still got more ground to cover."

They rode farther out from the camp, making sure to keep themselves out of the view of those other two. This time, Sandra was watching Ned closely as they patrolled. In a short amount of time, they were riding in step with one another, enjoying a night that most others would have thought to be hell on earth.

THIRTY-TWO

The night wore on, but as the snow fell in heavier gusts, the pale reflection of light grew steadily brighter. So much snow covered so many different surfaces that what little light there was reflected back and forth from one shiny surface to another. Although it was eerily beautiful, it brought with it a feeling of dread.

Looking around at the landscape of soft white curves and glittering drifts, Clint wondered only one thing. "How the hell are we going to get through this?"

"What's that?" LeAnne asked. "Do I sense a bit of pessimism from the great Gunsmith himself?"

Clint shook his head. "Oh no. Not at all. After breakfast, we should have plenty of time to build snowmen. Anyone have an old top hat?"

Rocking back and forth to keep the blood flowing, Mike held his hands out to the sputtering fire and rubbed them together. "You don't think we're gonna make it?"

There was no mistaking the despair in Mike's voice. The youngest member of the group had been holding his own so far, but he was not used to putting his life on the line. At that moment, Clint wished he had kept his question to himself.

"We're going to make it," Clint rectified. "We may just need to figure out some alternatives."

Mike turned and scooped up some of the thick, fluffy snow. "This doesn't seem too bad."

"Not right now, maybe," LeAnne said. "And not right here. But it's still coming down and we've got a cart to pull."

"All right, here's the plan," Clint said, since he knew that was what the moment called for. "We all take turns sleeping in the shelter while the other ones keep the fire going and keep the cart from getting too buried. That way, we should be rested and somewhat warm, and the work we'll have to do in the morning won't be so bad."

It was a simple plan, but Clint could see that it was having an effect on Mike. Already the younger man wasn't looking so grim, and in desperate times, that went a long way.

"Why don't you get some rest, Mike?" Clint said. "You've earned it."

"Naw, I can work first. I've been sitting in that damn seat all day anyhow."

"All right then," Clint said. "Let me put this another way. You rest first because I want to get my own work out of the way."

Mike smirked and nodded. "All right, Clint. You got it."

With that, Mike headed for the little tent and started bundling himself in blankets. In no time at all, the sound of loud snoring came rumbling out of the tent. Outside, Clint and LeAnne smiled at each other.

"He was exhausted," LeAnne said.

"I know. That's why I wanted him to rest first. He also needs to warm up."

"We all do."

"Yeah, but not all of us are getting close to freezing to death."

LeAnne looked at him with questioning eyes. "And Mike is?"

"He's getting lightheaded. You can see that in his eyes. His voice was sounding groggy, too. He needs to warm up, and the warmest place we've got is in that tent and under those blankets."

"Impressive," LeAnne said with a nod. "And here I thought Sandra and I were the experts in dealing with this cold."

"I've done my share of traveling. Maybe not as much in the cold as you two, but I've picked up some things along the way."

She looked at him approvingly, watching him for a little longer than the situation called for. Finally, she scooted in closer to him and dropped her voice to a whisper. "I've been thinking about something else that keeps me warm."

"Let me guess. Your toes?"

"No, but when I think about that night we had, it curls my toes all the same."

Images rushed through Clint's mind of the last night he'd shared with LeAnne in Krieger's Pass. Thoughts of naked skin and touching in the dark washed through him, leaving him a bit warmer as well. "That helps," he said, reaching out and placing his hand on her cheek before kissing her on the lips. "But a little of the real thing goes a long way."

"You're making me want to forget about my duties tonight, Clint Adams."

"Well," he said, getting to his feet and helping LeAnne onto hers, "we can't have that."

Before he could make another move, LeAnne slid her fingers over the back of Clint's neck and up into his hair while planting a kiss on him that curled the toes inside his boots. Once she felt that she'd made an impression, she pulled slowly away and said, "No, we can't."

She went to the fire and set a few more pieces of wood onto the flames, smirking as she saw the extra effort Clint threw into the job of clearing the snow from the cart's wheels.

THIRTY-THREE

The camp was dark, quiet. Only the roar of the wind and the patter of frozen pellets against the tree trunks broke the silence. Earlier, feet had crunched against the ground as the gang dragged various pieces of equipment from one spot to another. There wasn't much equipment to speak of, but the cold made the men's efforts all the more difficult as bones and joints became frozen together.

Burt was pitching in more than anyone, which made it so none of the men were willing to complain about the tasks they'd been assigned. Once the work was done, the only thing left was to sit tight and try to make it through the night.

And it was going to be a hell of a long night.

"You hear back from Jimmy?" Burt asked.

Frye was nearby. He was sitting next to a member of the gang that he'd thought was dead and buried already. Having reunited with the rest of the gang hours ago, Frye was glad to see faces other than Burt's. The leader was so intent on his goal that standing anywhere near him was like being beside a bundle of lit dynamite.

"Nobody's heard much of anything," Frye said without

133

getting up from his spot. "We should hear something soon, though."

"How many men did we send out?"

Frye looked over at Burt, unsure if the other man really needed him to answer or was just setting him up for some kind of test. But the look on Burt's face was genuine enough, if not a little frazzled. "Three groups of two."

"How long ago was that?"

"A couple hours. Are you all right, Burt?"

Burt's eyes darted over to Frye. They were filled with a wild, crazy fire that flared up and died down in the space of a second, a very scary second.

"I'm fine," Burt growled. "Don't worry about me. Just do what I tell you."

"Fine, fine." Allowing a couple seconds for the other man to cool off, Frye said, "Take a load off by the fire. There ain't anything you can see or hear over there that you can't right here."

For a moment, Burt looked like he might snap again. But then he inhaled and closed his eyes, holding his breath for a few seconds. When he exhaled and opened his eyes, the crazy fire was completely gone, replaced by something much more sedate.

Burt held his hands out and warmed them. As he stared into the flames, he seemed unaware of the world around him. The snow continued to fall, covering everyone with white powder. With nobody speaking, the wind's howl sounded even louder and the ice seemed to pelt the trees even harder.

"We can't sleep here," Burt said.

Frye looked around, checking to make sure that the men beside him had heard that as well. Judging by their confused expressions, Frye could only assume that they'd heard Burt just fine. Glancing back to Burt, Frye asked, "What did you say?"

"We can't sleep here. We need to keep moving."

"But if we don't get any sleep, we'll drop out of our saddles."

"Then get some shut-eye if you want, but it'll only be for a few hours. After that, we're heading out."

Frye could tell Burt was serious and that chilled him even through the frigid temperatures already surrounding him. Scooting closer to Burt, Frye spoke in a lowered voice so the others couldn't hear him.

"All due respect, Burt, but we can't go anywhere tonight. This storm's just getting started and if we try to find our way in the dark, we'll just wind up—"

"There ain't no dark," Burt said, the crazy fire in his eyes returning. "We can see just fine, which means we can travel just fine."

"But what about the men we sent out? How will they know where to find us?"

"Half of 'em are probably dead anyway and good riddance to 'em."

"Burt, you're not talking sense. You need to—"

"You don't tell me what I need! What we need is to catch up to that goddamn O'Connover before he gets across that border. Jesus Christ, I can't even believe we haven't taken them out by now."

"We will, but we can't do anything if we're too tired to move."

Burt stared at Frye for a few seconds. Frye recognized that a conflict was raging behind Burt's eyes. It looked almost as if Burt was listening to two sets of voices arguing inside of him. Every so often, his eyes would even dart one way and then another as if he could see the fight as clear as day.

Eventually Burt appeared to settle down and he looked straight at Frye. He nodded and reached out to snatch a bottle from one of the other men's hands. "Yeah," he said after taking a pull of whiskey. "You're right. We need our rest. Them others couldn't have gone too far from here."

"That's right. They put some distance between us, but there's no way they could have shaken us for good. No way in hell."

Burt nodded, but kept nodding for a little too long.

Frye couldn't decide if Burt was going over what he'd just heard or if he was listening to voices only he could hear. To be on the safe side, Frye decided to stay awake for as long as he could manage while keeping Burt at a safe distance.

He'd seen men driven out of their minds by fevers, their thoughts muddied by visions until they couldn't see straight. Those men sweated like pigs despite the cold, which was exactly what Burt was doing. Of course, Frye knew better than to suggest such a thing to the gang leader's face.

"I think Burt may be sick," one of the other men said to Frye after Burt had been staring at the same spot for over an hour.

"Yeah," Frye said simply. "Could be."

"What should we do?"

"We do what needs to be done. About Burt, O'Connover and Adams. With this storm wearing them down, all three of those problems will probably be solved real quick."

THIRTY-FOUR

Time lost its meaning when Mother Nature was throwing a fit. Whether it be rain, snow, heat or cold, everything else came to a stop to let nature take its course. It was hard to keep track of minutes when each one felt as if it could be your last. After a while, time stretched out or sped by so much that it became irrelevant.

It was getting close to dawn. It had been two days since Clint had seen a trace of Sandra or Ned. In that time, the group had kept themselves pointed north as they moved along as best they could.

The storm had yet to show a sign of letting up. Like a big old bear, it attacked them relentlessly. Snow fell in never-ending waves, and the ice formed layers on top of it all that broke under their feet like sheets of glass. The horses moved slower with each passing hour, and if the riders weren't trying to keep their own limbs from freezing to a standstill, they just might have noticed.

Rather than worry about the two missing from their party, Clint decided to stick to the path that they'd all agreed on at the beginning. At least that way Sandra and Ned would know where to look once they decided to catch up.

The one good thing that had happened since the onset of the storm was that Burt and his men had been fairly quiet. Clint didn't doubt that the gang was still out there, but he understood why any planned ambush had been put off: walking at a normal pace was tricky enough under those conditions; an ambush would be near impossible.

Another night had come and gone, dragging on as much as the ones before it. Their tasks had become routine and talk among the party was forced at best. For his part, O'Connover was behaving like the perfect passenger. After all, he was in the best shelter and not forced to do any work. LeAnne wouldn't allow him out of the cart no matter what she heard from anyone else.

Clint, LeAnne and Mike were all starting to wonder if they would ever see Sandra and Ned again. What should have been a scouting excursion had turned into two full nights away from camp. And when the nights were as deadly as those spent in the belly of the storm, it might as well have been a year.

The horses were wrapped in their blankets, and it was LeAnne's turn to sleep while Mike dug and Clint tended the fire. That gave Clint some time to sit and think about what might have befallen their two scouts. The more he thought about it, the more foolish he felt for having let them go off together. From a practical standpoint, if he lost them, he and the rest of his party might as well turn around and head back to Oregon.

As that grim thought went through his mind, Clint heard something he'd been praying the whole night that he wouldn't hear. It started as a shivering rumble that came from deep within one of the horses' throats. When he turned around to look at the animals standing close together for warmth, Clint saw it was the horse normally hooked to the cart that had made the noise.

That horse was shivering and shaking its head while shifting from one foot to another. Clint went over to figure out what was wrong but already knew what he'd find. The animal's eyes were wild and glassy as though it had just lost its vision. When Clint reached out to pat its neck, its skin felt sticky and the animal was twitching.

In a matter of minutes, the animal could no longer hold its head up and then finally toppled over. Eclipse stood next to it and stepped aside when he felt the other's weight against him, allowing the cart horse to drop to the ground. The sound of the large body hitting the earth was loud enough to bring Mike over from his work.

"What happened?" he asked. "Is she all right?"

Clint had his hand on the horse's neck and let out a deep breath. "She's dead. The cold got to her."

"Aw, shit. I thought for sure she'd make it through this. She's made it through worse."

Clint checked the horse's blankets and found everything to be tied up as well as it could have been. "Well, it happens. There's a reason people stay home when storms like this pass through and this is one of them. We're lucky this didn't happen to one of us instead of this horse."

"Yeah," Mike said, bending down to put his hand on the side of the horse's head. "I guess."

Without another word, Clint and Mike pulled the dead horse's blanket up over its head. The falling snow quickly buried the animal. With the storm still rolling through and plenty more work still to be done, there wasn't much else they could do for that horse.

Out on the trail, a horse was not just another animal. No matter what, a horse was the life of its rider. Even if the animal was only pulling a cart, it was still a vital piece of the group: none of the two-legged members could pull that wagon.

"Should we get moving?" Mike asked as the sun started to poke through the thick layers of clouds overhead.

Clint felt as though he'd been in that damn snow for months. He was cold down to the bone and tired as hell despite the few hours of sleep he'd managed to get. "Not just yet. We'll let LeAnne sleep for another hour. Hopefully, we'll see Sandra or Ned by then."

"And what if we don't hear anything from them?"

Clint sat down in front of the fire he'd been tending and watched as a gust of wind threatened to blow out the last sputtering flame. He was too frozen to scramble for more wood and too tired to give a damn.

"If we don't see them by then," Clint said, "we'll keep an eye out for them when we head out. They know where we're headed, and if anyone could catch up to us, it's them."

Mike opened his mouth to ask another question, but realizing it would be the same question as his last one, he shut his mouth instead.

They both sat there staring at the logs that had only moments ago been their fire but were now covered in snow. It felt good to sit still. But more than anything, they wanted to lie down and get some sleep.

THIRTY-FIVE

Having spent so much time together, Sandra and Ned rarely needed to speak to communicate with one another. Each had grown accustomed to the other's looks, movements and patterns so much so that the pair functioned like a well-oiled machine despite the brutal surroundings.

Since they'd parted from the others, they'd tracked one small group of gang members after another. Between tracking the gang and fighting to maintain the finely tuned habits they'd developed of moving while staying out of sight, they hardly noticed as one day slipped into another.

They'd made their peace with the storm and now treated it as though it were just another turn of the weather. At the first light of this dawn, Sandra lay beneath the little shelter that Ned kept in his bedroll. It wasn't much more than half a tent, just big enough to cover them both so long as they were both lying down.

Instead of normal saddlebags, Sandra used a rolled-up leather bundle that was actually a bear's hide that had been tanned and fashioned into a large square. Once unrolled and spread out, the hide revealed the soft, thick bear fur that made the square one of the warmest blankets Sandra had ever known.

It was warm enough to shield her from the extremes of the storm and tough enough to become more comforting with every passing year. And, as a blanket, it was big enough to wrap around two people. Of course, it helped if those two people were lying as close as Sandra and Ned now were.

The first night, they'd slept separately even though they'd grown closer while hunting the gang. As they learned more about each other, a bond developed between them until there was only one way for them to get closer.

They greeted this morning as they had the one before, wrapped in the thick bear skin and entwined in each other's arms. Their clothes lay in a pile nearby, covered in a layer of snow and marked with a twig sticking straight up from the ground. They were covered with snow as well, beneath Ned's tent. But under the tent and under the skin, they were warmer than any other living thing for miles around.

Sandra's strong legs wrapped around Ned's body, holding him tight while pulling him closer. Ned's arms were wrapped around her, pressing her firm breasts against his chest as he ran his fingers along the small of her back and up and down the curve of her buttocks. As his hands moved along her body, Ned could feel her squirming against him.

The rigid shaft of Ned's cock glided between Sandra's legs, brushing against the lips of her pussy and bringing urgent moans from the back of her throat. Though she wanted him inside of her, Sandra wasn't about to rush it. The feel of his hard penis between her legs sent chills down her spine that had nothing to do with the cold.

Ned could feel her getting wetter each time he rubbed against her clitoris. Sandra's nails dug into him as she arched her back, pushing her lower body against him even harder. He needed only to push against her in a certain way for him to let her know what he wanted. The same bond that allowed them to track and hunt together without saying a word also made them perfect lovers.

They'd both felt that, even before the first time he'd entered her. Now that they were reveling in each other's arms, they let instinct guide every motion, and each time was better than the last.

Sandra shifted her hips, allowing Ned to bury himself inside of her. Her entire body clenched as she took him in. She opened her eyes only when she felt filled by him, and when she tried to take a breath, it was quickly taken away as he began thrusting in and out.

Moving both hands down to cup her backside, Ned squeezed her tight curves while guiding her as he thrust between her legs. Every inch of his naked body was feeling either her smooth skin or the soft fur of the blanket wrapped around them. At first, Sandra's body moved to conform to his, easing away as he pulled out and pushing against him in anticipation of every thrust. They'd both grown so accustomed to moving with absolute quiet that even the moans she made were soft and low, intended only for Ned's ears.

Soon, Ned felt her body no longer moving so fluidly with his. Reading that signal perfectly, he eased off and allowed her to twist herself until she was lying on top of him. Still wrapped in the bear skin, they enjoyed the feel of the other for a few minutes without moving.

Ned felt himself growing even harder beneath the warm weight of her body, and Sandra ground herself against him, knowing right where he wanted to be touched. Lifting herself up slightly, she arched her back again, straddling his cock while sliding down along its length and letting her hard nipples brush against his chest.

Stretching her arms out so she could reach out past Ned's head, Sandra clenched her fingers around the edge of the bear skin. Ned moved his hands up along her back so he could cup both her breasts and massage them gently yet firmly.

Sandra shut her eyes tightly and started riding him. Her pussy fit perfectly around him, gliding down his shaft and then easing back up again. As her rhythm picked up, Ned added more to it by pumping his hips slightly every time she came down.

Their bodies rocked back and forth, her on top of him and then him rolling on top of her. When her back was pressed down against the blanket and she felt his weight on top of her, Sandra let out a contented moan and spread her legs open a little wider for him. Ned's cock slid into place easily, driving all the way inside of her until their bodies were pressed tightly against one another.

Ned shifted slightly, just enough to feel his chest push against her breasts. He moved his hands up and down her sides, enjoying the way she felt beneath him and the way she would squirm when he touched one of her favorite spots. Eventually, Ned moved his hands up along the sides of her breasts and kept on going until one hand slid through her thick hair and the other ran up along the arm that she extended out of the blanket.

Closing his hand around hers, Ned began rocking back and forth while slowly gliding in and out between her legs. Every time he eased upward, he came out of her almost completely. That made it all the better when he pushed back into her, allowing his entire length to slip between the lips of her vagina.

With a shift of his weight and a slight adjustment to his movement, Ned started rubbing his cock against her clit as he entered her. That alone was enough to make her eyes go wide with pleasure and her breath to start coming in short, passionate bursts.

Sandra tightened her grip around his hand and clenched her eyes shut. She wrapped her legs around him, which gave him better access to her most sensitive area. Her entire body started to tremble with the approaching climax and her moans grew louder and louder. Giving into the desires that coursed through her, Sandra reached down with both hands under the blanket to grab Ned's hips and pull him into her even harder.

Not one to argue with a lady, Ned took her direction perfectly and added to it with a circular movement that brushed his rigid penis against even more spots that sent shivers through her skin. As her orgasm took hold of her, all of Sandra's muscles clenched, making her pussy even tighter around his column of flesh.

Now it was Ned's turn to feel the pleasure ripple beneath his skin. With Sandra thrashing beneath him in the powerful hold of her own climax, Ned pumped into her faster and harder to intensify his own. Not only did it give him a sensation so intense it made him dizzy, but it brought a little cry from the back of Sandra's throat.

After catching his breath, Ned ran a finger down Sandra's face and stopped with it over her lips. "Shhh," he whispered. "We don't want anyone to know we're here, remember?"

Sandra gave him a wicked smile, opened her lips and flicked her tongue against his finger. "Of course I remember. That's what makes these times we have together so amazing."

"That was pretty amazing, wasn't it?" Ned asked, bringing his hips to a stop while keeping himself inside of her.

"Don't get too full of yourself. It takes two, you know."

"I know. Hell, I've been thinking about what the two of us could do together since the moment I laid eyes on you. I just thought you couldn't stand the sight of me."

The wicked smile stayed on Sandra's face when she said, "I couldn't. You just grew on me. Like a fungus."

"A fungus, huh? I'll show you a—"

Ned stopped as a sound in the distance caught their attention. Their eyes darted to the same spot as both of their bodies became completely still. Ned could feel Sandra's muscles tensing beneath him and couldn't help but take a look down at her finely honed curves.

"Sounds like they're on the move again," Sandra said in a voice almost too low to be a whisper. "We've got to get going."

"Yeah," Ned grunted as he started to get up. "All good things gotta end sometime."

THIRTY-SIX

The day couldn't have started any worse. Not only had they lost the horse meant to pull the cart, but Clint was also having a hell of a time finding a suitable replacement. Because of their diligence in keeping the cart dug out overnight, they'd managed to get it rolling using Le-Anne's horse. But her mare was built for speed: although it was working through the cold, it just didn't have the strength to pull a wagon as well as everything else in it.

The weather conditions compounded the problem. The longer the snow had fallen, the more solidly it had become packed on the ground. To top it all off, just enough ice had formed to hold everything together like mortar.

The situation left Clint with only one choice and he wasn't too happy about it.

"All right, boy," Clint said, patting Eclipse on the neck. "Looks like you're going to have to pull a little more than your own weight for a while."

The Darley Arabian took the place of LeAnne's mare at the front of the cart. He bristled a bit at the unfamiliar feeling of being attached to such a rig, but it wasn't long before he was accepting Clint's instruction at the reins.

Even with the wheels turning and the cart rolling, Clint

could tell that Eclipse was having a hard time pulling the cart, its driver and the prisoner as well as Mike, who was sitting next to Clint in the seat.

"Hey Mike," Clint said to the younger man beside him. "Why don't you do me a favor and jump down from there."

Mike's eyes narrowed as Clint brought the cart to a halt. "What? You want me to walk?"

"No. I want you to let O'Connover out of his warm little box so he can walk along beside the cart. That'll be less weight for Eclipse to pull."

LeAnne was riding in front of the cart and brought her horse around quickly when she heard Clint's words. "Oh no you don't. I went through too much trouble tracking that asshole down and dragging him this far just to give him a chance to get away now."

"Then you can chain him to the cart so we can pull him along," Clint replied. "Losing one horse is bad enough. I don't want to lose another one, and I'd rather lose ten O'Connovers than take a chance of losing Eclipse."

LeAnne shifted her eyes from Clint to the cart to the Darley Arabian pulling it. Being someone who was more than familiar with the life bond that formed between certain horses and their riders, she finally nodded. "All right then, but I'm riding where I can keep an eye on him."

"Sounds fine to me," Clint said. Pointing ahead to terrain that displayed fewer trees and more open land, he added, "Even if he did get away from us, there aren't many places for him to go where we can't see him."

Grudgingly, LeAnne agreed, and she took it upon herself to drag O'Connover out of the cart and rearrange his chains so whatever slack she was forced to give him around his ankles was made up around his wrists. She not only bound him to the back of the cart, but she also

threaded one chain through a ring on the side, forcing
O'Connover to walk on the left.

Clint watched as LeAnne went about the task of handling O'Connover and saw why Bobby was so content to
let her go on this trip without him. She handled herself
with strength and confidence, not giving O'Connover one
inch of breathing room, tying him so tightly to the cart
that it was practically a part of him.

"All right," Clint said, flicking Eclipse's reins from the
driver's seat. "I'd suggest you keep up unless you want
your backside to get real acquainted with the ground."

As always, O'Connover carried on without saying
more than two words at a time. Although he didn't look
happy to be in the elements, he clearly appreciated being
able to stretch his legs after several days of being stuck
away like an old blanket.

With their party rearranged, and despite its peculiar
appearance, they immediately covered more ground. Being in the storm was like being under a giant's slow-
moving boot: it crushed down upon them with
overwhelming power, but it was a constant weight that
they'd slowly learned to bear.

It took some time for them to realize that the weight
was easing up. Throughout the first part of the day, Clint
as well as all the others started looking up more fre-
quently. It was a simple gesture, perhaps, but one that
hadn't been an option earlier because doing so would have
resulted in a face full of ice.

Now, however, they could actually see some blue between the shreds of gray clouds, and enough sunlight was
streaming through to do more than just show them the
way. When they rolled into an area bathed in sunlight,
Clint wasn't the only one who needed to take a minute
or two to let his eyes adjust.

For the next hour or so, they were all as disoriented as
Clint had been when he'd first encountered the wintry

elements. They soon got their bearings, however, and everyone was looking around with smiles on their faces and a spring in their step.

"I don't want to jinx us," Mike said, "but I think we may be out of the storm for good."

Clint looked up and studied the sky. Not only were the clouds directly overhead thinning out, but the sky in front of them looked practically clear. "Yeah," he said with a happy nod. "I'd guess it's safe to celebrate. It's clearing up enough for me to get a fix on where the hell we are. Until now, all I could tell was which direction we were facing."

"We're about another two days ride from where we need to be," LeAnne said with certainty.

"Are you sure about that?" Clint asked.

"Yep. While you two were feeling the sun on your faces, I've been looking for landmarks. I've made this run enough times to recognize this view. We should be crossing over the border tomorrow night if we're lucky, but that doesn't mean it's going to be easy."

"I'm the one driving this cart," Clint said. "You don't have to tell me there's still too much snow and ice beneath us to go any faster than a snail's pace. But still, it beats the hell out of freezing to death in the middle of the night."

Clint saw LeAnne and Mike twitch in response to his comment. He knew they were all thinking the same thing with regard to freezing to death: they still hadn't heard back from Ned or Sandra and they were slowly putting those woods behind them.

THIRTY-SEVEN

They were no longer surrounded by trees, but the terrain was still uneven and plenty of rock faces jutted up from the ground at odd angles. Before too long, Clint was fairly certain of their position and he thought LeAnne's estimate of their arrival time, although a bit optimistic, was pretty much correct.

Still, even without the storm to deal with, he felt as if he was making the entire ride while holding his breath. He knew more challenges awaited them before the job was through. Part of him wanted to complete the journey safely, but another part of him wanted that other shoe just to go ahead and drop. Thinking about that dark unknown dangling over their heads, Clint looked down to O'Connover, who was doing a fairly good job of keeping up with the cart.

"You remember what you said a while ago?" Clint asked. "About Burt wanting to kill you rather than free you?"

"Jesus Christ," LeAnne groaned. "Not this bullshit again. I don't know how many times I had to listen to that when I was bringing him in. Don't listen to him,

Clint. He's just trying to throw you off with a mouthful of lies."

Clint kept his eyes on O'Connover and waited until LeAnne was finished. When it was obvious that he wasn't about to respond to her, Clint said, "You remember that, O'Connover?"

O'Connover glanced up at Clint and then looked back down to his own shuffling feet. "Yeah."

"You want to finish up what you were saying?"

Without lifting his eyes from where they were focused on the ground directly in front of him, O'Connover replied, "No. There ain't no use anyhow."

"Why not? I'm willing to listen. There's still a ways to go and I haven't heard this before."

"Because whether you listen or not, it's too late. Either I'll be going to Canada to die or I'll be killed out here before I get there. It's too late to fix things now."

"Fix what things?"

"You just won't let this go, will you, Adams?"

Clint put an easy smile on his face and shook his head. "Nope."

For the next several steps, O'Connover kept his head down and acted as if Clint and the others had simply disappeared. But when he took a quick look up again, he found Clint still staring down at him, wearing that same easygoing smile.

"All right, for Christ's sake," O'Connover grunted. "You want to hear it, then I'll tell you just like I told everyone else before you. Do you know any lawmen up north of the border?"

The question caught Clint off guard and he had to think a minute or two before answering it. "I've met a few here and there over the years."

"Well, if you could get them all together and ask them about the men you're delivering me to, I guarantee you they wouldn't know who the hell these men are. You know why that is?"

"No," LeAnne interrupted, "but you're sure as hell going to tell us."

"Yeah, I am going to tell you. He wants to hear it, so he's going to hear it."

Before LeAnne could say anything more, Clint stopped her with a polite yet firm raised hand. "Let him say his piece, LeAnne. I want to hear it."

Frozen with more scalding words still on the tip of her tongue, LeAnne let out an aggravated breath. After an exaggerated roll of her eyes, she waved her arm and bowed sarcastically before flicking her reins and moving a few paces ahead of the cart.

"Go on," Clint said.

"Those men that put the price on my head ain't the law," O'Connover explained.

"But it's a legal bounty, isn't it?" Clint's confidence came from the fact that he was certain Bobby Hill wouldn't have put him through all of this under false pretenses. The man might have had his questionable moments, but he wasn't the kind to do that to a friend.

"I'm sure it is legal," O'Connover said, putting one of Clint's worries to rest. "But the men who set the price have enough lawmen on their payroll to arrange a bounty on a nobody like me. All they did was put up the cash and pay for the fancy paper. That way, they get me delivered to them with no questions asked by fortune hunters like your friends here."

Clint didn't flinch at the way O'Connover talked about the others as though the words themselves were dipped in shit. Instead, he shrugged and asked, "So you're an innocent man? You told me back in Krieger's Pass that you've stolen and fired a gun or two, so which is it?"

"All that's true, but I never did anything as god-awful as what's been spread around about me."

"Then why the bounty?"

"Because the men who set that price want me dead but only after they manage to get me out in the middle of nowhere so they can take their time questioning me. Bounty hunters do their delivery work pretty damn well and they don't ask questions. The men that are after me don't want any more people knowing about them than already do.

"Do you know how much unclaimed land is up north, Mister Adams? Do you have any idea how many prospecting companies are interested in digging for everything from gold to silver to coal up there?"

Although he didn't know exact figures, Clint knew well enough just how far greed could take a man. He'd had plenty of firsthand experience watching rich men's struggles to get even richer, so his own observations lent a fair amount of credence to what O'Connover was saying.

"I can imagine," was all Clint said in reply.

"Well, take whatever you just imagined and double it," O'Connover said. "Maybe then you can get an idea of what we're talking about."

"So what?" Mike said. "There's plenty to be dug up out of the ground in this country. What makes you or these other fellas you're talking about so special?"

"The difference is that we're here and they're across the border. Things work different up north. There're trappers up there who practically run their own towns just because they don't leave when the snows come. There's more up for grabs and some folks aren't so civilized in how they do their grabbing.

"It's not lawless, but it's a hell of a lot wilder than we're used to sometimes. What makes this so special is that these businessmen aren't exactly your more reputable types."

Shifting his eyes over to LeAnne, O'Connover asked,

"How many bounties have you lost because they managed to get away from you by slipping south to Mexico or north into Canada?"

LeAnne didn't answer. She was too busy sulking.

Whether she responded to him or not, O'Connover was rolling and he wasn't about to stop now. "What did you think they all did once they got out of the country and away from hunters like you?" he asked. "Farming? Maybe open a nice little shop?"

"Actually," Clint put in, "some of them do just that."

O'Connover looked up at him and said, "Yeah, and some of them wait for enough like-minded fellows to join them so they can start brewing something up that'll make them some real money."

"How do you know all of this?" Clint asked.

"Because I used to be one of them. Well, one of the hired hands, anyway. I knew a man by the name of Owen Mays. He used to find work for me when I was still knocking over stagecoaches and shooting poker cheats for five bucks a head."

Clint's stomach clenched. "Owen Mays? Now, I've heard of that one."

"I'll bet you have. Well, he'd been out of the picture for some time, and a year ago, I got a letter from him telling me that if I'd come up north to lend a hand with what he had working in Canada, he'd vouch for me. I was broke, so I rode up there with nothing to lose.

"Owen never was much good, but he and the others he joined with were worse than I could've ever guessed. They're rich too. All of 'em. They got that way by taking over mines they stole from prospectors, running towns they had overtaken after killing off all the law and eventually starting up a company of their own with all the profits. Hell, there's more, but I don't have enough breath to list off all they were into."

"So Mays is behind all of this?" Clint asked.

"Some of it. About a dozen others that work with him are behind even more. They all have men working for them that're loyal to them from their days in the States. Now that they're all rich, Mays's inner circle are looking for more. Since they each have their own bunch ready to take orders, all they need to do is knock Mays from the top spot."

"So where do you come in?" Clint asked.

O'Connover shrugged and let his head droop down as though he'd suddenly lost the strength to hold it up. His reply was cut short by the sound of horses racing up to them from behind and to the right.

Turning to look at who was coming, Clint wore an expectant smile on his face. "Is that Ned and Sandra?"

But LeAnne didn't look happy and Clint's smile was already fading.

"If it is," she said, "they're bringing company."

THIRTY-EIGHT

"I count three of them," Clint said, dividing his attention between driving the cart and looking back over his shoulder.

Mike had already snatched the rifle from under the cart's seat and was checking to make sure it was ready to fire. After squinting toward the sound of oncoming horses, he said, "Make that four."

Sure enough, when Clint turned to get another look, he saw that one of the figures he'd seen before was hiding another who had now ridden around to become a shape all its own. "Dammit," he snarled under his breath while snapping the reins again.

Eclipse responded as much to Clint's voice as he did to the touch of leather on his back. Digging his hooves into the packed snow beneath them, the Darley Arabian put all his muscle into each step to get that cart moving faster.

"LeAnne," Clint shouted. "I need you to—"

Suddenly, a shot blasted from Clint's left. It was so close he practically jumped from his skin. Clint hadn't seen any possible threats coming from that direction, and the shot sounded as though it had been fired from only a foot or two away.

A million thoughts rolled through Clint's mind. He cursed himself for not seeing whoever it was that had taken that shot, and he wondered if that one stupid mistake might just end his life. He even wondered if his own gun had somehow gone off by mistake.

Then he wondered why LeAnne would take a shot at him when he'd thought for sure she was on his side.

That last thought came when he saw LeAnne falling back to ride closer to the cart. She held a smoking pistol in her hand and was already taking another shot. In an instant, Clint realized that neither shot was aimed at him but at the side of the cart itself.

Clint's ears also picked up the sound of jangling chains knocking against the side of the cart. LeAnne's second shot sparked against metal as well, and with her free hand, she reached down to scoop up the man who'd been locked into those chains.

O'Connover's face was covered in sweat, the result of pumping his legs to try to keep up with the cart that had taken off with him still attached to it. He grabbed at LeAnne's saddle and scrambled upward while she pulled him along. Their combined efforts allowed him to get onto the horse's back before he lost his footing.

Looking over to Clint, LeAnne asked, "What do you need me to do?"

"Actually, you just did it. Next time, warn me before firing a gun in my direction, all right?"

"Will do, but I think you may have to worry about them firing at you first."

"Don't worry about them," Mike said. "You two just worry about keeping those horses moving. It's about time I earned my share around here."

Before anyone could say anything else, Mike levered a round into his rifle and stood up on the driver's seat of the cart. He kept his balance long enough to get himself turned around and facing the oncoming riders. Lying flat on his belly along the top of the cart, Mike pressed the rifle stock against his shoulder and sighted down the barrel.

Clint could hear the riders getting closer, and he could also hear enough of their shouts to one another to know that they meant to split up and surround the cart.

A gunshot rang out from the distance, which was answered almost instantly by a shot from Mike's rifle. Lead hissed through the air as more and more shots were fired. The majority of bullets were coming from the riders, but Clint was relieved to know that Mike wasn't firing wildly and expending all his ammunition.

"What're you—?" O'Connover shouted while holding on for dear life as he lay across LeAnne's saddle. "Aw, Jesus!"

The prisoner's loud complaints came from the fact that, rather than trying to get him away from the gunfire, LeAnne seemed intent on taking him closer to it. As much as he wanted to fight or get the hell away from there, O'Connover was in the position to do neither. He could only grit his teeth and hang on, white-knuckled, for dear life.

LeAnne pulled back on her reins just enough to get a few paces back from the cart. From there, she twisted around to take a look at the riders as they rushed in on her from two sides. The gang had already split to surround the cart, so she took aim at the closest ones she could find.

She managed to squeeze off one shot before one of the oncoming riders singled her out and returned fire. The first bullet hissed past LeAnne, only close enough to make her twitch. The second shot came a lot closer, shredding a section of her right sleeve and digging out a messy trench in her flesh.

Clint was dividing his attention between the fight going on behind him and the road in front of Eclipse. As much as he wanted to draw his Colt and join in the scuffle, he didn't dare. He trusted Eclipse more than he did most people, but the stallion was taking orders from Clint and was depending on his guidance at the reins.

"Shit!" Clint cursed as he ducked his head under the incoming bullets sizzling around him.

"Yeah," Mike said, his voice surprisingly calm even as he levered in another round and fired it off. "I was just thinking the same thing."

"Are those shooters getting closer?" Clint asked.

Mike took careful aim and fired. This time, Clint heard the distinct sound of a man hollering before something heavy hit the ground. "It's not exactly these shooters I was thinking about."

"What?"

"I was more concerned about them."

Clint glanced back again and saw Mike pointing off toward a little stand of trees they'd just passed. Following that line of sight, Clint quickly spotted another pair of riders exploding from the trees and heading toward them like charging bulls.

"Aw hell," Clint grunted.

THIRTY-NINE

Clint knew that Eclipse was a strong horse, but even the strongest of God's creatures had its limits. Having seen what happened when one of their horses was pushed past its own limit, Clint was more than a little reluctant to push Eclipse past his. But these were desperate times, so Clint cringed and offered up a little apology under his breath as he snapped the reins and demanded the Darley Arabian to pull the cart even faster.

The stallion complied, not without a few loud replies of his own, however. Nevertheless, Eclipse complied to such a degree that the cart began bouncing over every bump in the road, speeding along as though it might fly off the face of the earth at any second.

All around them, the shooting carried on. In addition to the two riders Mike and Clint had spotted coming from the trees, another three were barrelling toward them fast on the heels of the first bunch.

"Got another one," LeAnne shouted as the man she'd been picking apart finally dropped from his saddle.

Clint was keeping track as best he could in his own head and figured that at least half of the first wave of riders were down. Of course, enough reinforcements were charging at them to at least replenish the original number and then some. Rather than trying to work out the totals, Clint focused on driving the cart.

"There's more on their way," Mike said as if reading Clint's thoughts. "They're getting closer, and we won't be able to do much about it since we're dragging this heap."

"Yeah, well this heap has all our supplies in it, so we'd better keep it with us."

Mike took one more shot and rolled onto his side. "Reach under that seat and see if you can find the box of shells for this thing."

Doing his best to look for the shells while watching the road and driving the cart, Clint twisted himself around until his arm was at such an uncomfortable angle that it felt as if it might snap. Finally, his fingers brushed against a small box that gave off a familiar rattle when jostled.

"Here," Clint said as he handed over the box of shells. "Now where are those other riders?"

Mike quickly reloaded his rifle while casting his eyes around at the chaos surrounding his position. "Them other two'll be on us any second. Them others won't be too far behind 'em."

Before Clint could turn to look for himself, the two riders who'd emerged from the trees were upon him. He could feel them even before he heard the rumble of hooves, much as a mouse could feel a chill in its bones before being snatched up by a hawk.

The pair of horses were moving like a shot from a cannon, and hearing them rush toward him, Clint reached reflexively for the Colt at his side. Those instincts were checked, however, when he caught a passing glimpse at one of the rider's faces.

"Holy shit, I don't believe it!" Clint said.

Mike turned to look, bringing the rifle around as he did. He was just in time to see the pair of riders thunder directly toward the cart and then roar right past it. He got a look at them as well and was just as surprised to see Sandra and Ned sitting in those horses' saddles.

"Hot damn, it's the cavalry!" Mike shouted before shifting his aim to the other side of the cart where LeAnne was still doing her best to dodge bullets.

Only two men from the first charge were still in their saddles, one of whom was currently at the business end of LeAnne's barrel. She gritted her teeth and pulled her trigger, sending that gang member straight to hell with one well-placed shot through his skull.

The other man was coming up fast, getting so close to her that she could make out nearly every red whisker on his ratlike face. Snapping her gun toward him, LeAnne rolled with her instincts and pulled her trigger without waiting to take aim. Her instincts were quick and her aim was dead-on. Her gun, however, was empty.

Glaring at her with a triumphant smile, Frye dug his heels into his horse's sides to bring himself even closer to her. He chanced one look over his shoulder and when he saw the second wave of the ambush was under way, his smile became that much wider.

"Stay down," LeAnne said to O'Connover, who was still curled up across her saddle. With that as her only warning, LeAnne cocked her gun arm back and swung it out toward Frye's smirking face.

The other man leaned back but not quite far enough: the top edge of LeAnne's pistol cracked him across the cheekbone. His head was knocked back a bit, but any pain he might have felt was absorbed by the rush of adrenalin pumping through his system.

Expecting her to make another similar move, Frye baited LeAnne by sticking his jaw out; he didn't have to wait long before she reacted. He saw the swing coming and reached out to block the incoming steel with an open palm. His fingers closed around her fist as well as the gun itself.

He had only to pull and she would be knocked to the ground. Frye knew damn well that if the drop didn't break her neck, then she would probably be trampled by one of the horses nearby.

With that image in his mind, Frye tensed his muscles and started tugging LeAnne forward. Then a shot blasted through the air nearby. His ears still ringing, Frye felt a bullet tear through his shoulder like a hot talon ripping his flesh.

The moment she saw Frye recoil, LeAnne holstered her pistol and snapped her reins. She placed one hand on O'Connover's back to steady him as she urged her horse away from Frye. Within a few seconds, she was ahead of Eclipse.

Clint was watching her and was impressed at LeAnne's riding. Now that she and O'Connover were away from Frye, Clint intended to protect them both even if it meant steering the cart with the reins clenched in his teeth.

Rather than chase after LeAnne, Frye fell back a bit and pulled a shotgun from a holster on his saddle. He aimed both barrels at the cart and pulled both triggers, blasting out about half of the spokes on the cart's front wheel.

Suddenly the cart started to pitch and wobble. Clint could feel the wheel breaking away, his control over the cart fading with every splinter that fell from the wheel.

"Mike, we're in trouble," Clint shouted over the rattle and snapping of breaking wood. "Lots of it."

FORTY

Despite the pain that was starting to work its way through his body, Frye was still grinning. He shifted the reins to the same hand gripping the shotgun so he could snap it open and shove two fresh shells into the breech. He flicked it shut with a crack of his wrist and took aim at the already damaged cart wheel.

A shot blasted through the air and a chunk of hot lead dug a messy tunnel through Frye's chest. The wound in his shoulder was already making it a trial to hold his arm up, but this wound was something else entirely. As he started to lose sensation in his lower body, Frye looked straight into the eyes of the man who'd just shot him.

This time, it was Mike who wore the smile.

With the world starting to go black around the edges, Frye willed his body to go through one last set of motions. It wasn't to obey orders or even to please his gang's leader that Frye took aim at that wheel. He did so out of pure spite, to get one last dig at the man who'd ended his life. Using the last bit of strength in his body, Frye squeezed his trigger and emptied the shotgun's barrels. It was the last sound he heard before falling from his saddle.

He was dead before he even touched the ground.

The thud of Frye's body hitting the ground was drowned out by the deafening crackle of wood twisting itself into splinters. Frye's last shot had found its mark, and the only thing left of the wheel was a hub and a few trembling spokes. The metal rim was coming off and the rest of the wheel was just a mess of useless lumber.

A burst of panic surged through Clint. But rather than turning into fear and spinning him out of control right along with the cart, the sensation launched Clint into action. Without a word, he dropped the reins and reached down to find the pin that fastened Eclipse to the cart.

One pull was all it took to separate the broken cart from the Darley Arabian struggling to keep it moving. As soon as he saw Eclipse was free, Clint let out a powerful whistle that nearly drained every bit of air from his lungs.

Mike was still lying on his stomach on top of the cart. No longer firing off shots from the rifle, he was trying desperately to hold on and not get thrown from the cart. Although he knew he'd be tossed off no matter what, Mike maintained his grip simply because he didn't know what else to do.

The first thing Mike felt was the cart wrenching beneath him in the exact way he'd been dreading. Then he felt something slap against his back and his shirt collar tightening around his neck.

Before Mike could figure out what was happening, he was being lifted—not thrown, as he'd expected—off of the cart.

"Come on," Clint shouted while picking up Mike by the back of his shirt and jacket. "Time to get off this thing."

Mike's feet scrambled reflexively beneath him until his boots finally found purchase on top of the unsteady cart. With Clint pulling and pushing him toward the side of the cart, he threw himself in that direction, praying that Clint knew what the hell he was doing.

Using one hand to direct Mike and the other to keep his balance, Clint let out one more whistle and kept moving toward the side of the cart, which, in that moment, seemed impossibly far away. Everything else seemed to slow down around him as Clint stepped onto the edge of the cart just as the entire thing started to pitch over onto its side.

The cart had already driven its busted wheel into the ground and the rest of its momentum was carrying it into a complete flip. On top of the cart, both men churned their feet forward as if trying to stay on top of a giant rolling log.

Seeing Eclipse running toward them in response to the whistles was one of the most glorious sights Clint had seen in a long time. With one last shove, both men pushed off of the cart just as it flipped upside down into the air.

Clint felt his muscles burning under his skin from the strain of his jump, but it was all worthwhile as he landed roughly in the Darley Arabian's saddle. His left boot found the stirrups first, which gave him something to anchor himself to.

He needed all the anchoring he could get because he was now being pulled from Eclipse's back by a sudden, powerful tug that damn near ripped his arm from its socket. Mike hadn't been so lucky in his own jump and had managed only to clip Eclipse's back with his heels. From there, Mike kept right on falling. A fraction of a second before he was on the ground, he realized the hard way that Clint still had a hold of the back of his jacket.

Clint pulled Mike upward with as much strength as he could muster, but the effort sent a powerful wave of pain coursing from his shoulder down through his entire body. Fighting his way through the agony stabbing into his side, Clint yanked Mike up an inch or so, which was as far as he could manage.

Mike's hand shot out to grab hold of Clint. His boots

dragged along the ground as chunks of solid snow and ice slammed against him like boulders. When his heels bounced off the ground again, Mike used the momentum to swing his leg up and onto Eclipse's back. Another bounce nearly sent him face-first to the ground, but he pushed up with his knee, which was just enough to get him onto the horse's back all the way.

Once there, Mike held tight to Clint and fought to catch his breath.

"I knew Eclipse was originally a show horse," Clint said as the cart rolled and broke apart behind him, "but I never thought I'd be the one to pull off a trick like that."

"I'll buy a drink for the trainer when this is done," Mike replied.

"Yeah, but first there's business to settle." With that, Clint turned Eclipse around to face back toward the ambushers. He snapped the reins, drew his Colt and charged into the fray.

FORTY-ONE

Though he could see the smoke as well as the occasional gout of fire coming from the gunshots, Clint still couldn't hear them. The clamor from the cart rolling end over end was still a low rumble in his ears and his heartbeat was like a fist slamming against his eardrums. But he didn't need to hear the shots to find them. All he had to do was steer Eclipse toward the chaos.

As he and Mike got closer, however, that same chaos started to die away. Finally, as he approached pistol range, he saw a few shapes break off from the rest and head back toward the trees from which they'd come. That left only three riders in the swirling smoke, each one of them shifting around restlessly while looking for another target.

More than once, Eclipse had to sidestep what, at first, appeared to be a fallen log or snow-covered bump in the road. Several of those bumps were bodies that had fallen to the ground and rolled in the snow before coming to their final rest.

"It's great to see you two!" Clint shouted as he rode closer to where Ned and Sandra's horses were standing. "We were beginning to think the worst."

Ned put on his familiar half-cocked smile and, once

Clint was close enough, reached out to slap him on the back. "We stayed away a little longer than planned, but you gotta have faith, Adams."

Clint looked over to Sandra and found her cheeks flushed with the thrill of the chase. "If I didn't know any better, I'd say you two went off to grab some relaxation time. You look more rested than all of the rest of us combined."

His words were meant in jest, but Clint saw by the quick glimpse Sandra and Ned gave to each other that he'd actually touched on something a little deeper. Clint was not the expert tracker or hunter that the others in the group were, but he knew what that look meant when it passed between a man and a woman.

"I never was too good around a lot of people," Sandra said. "Being out there in the thick of things felt pretty good. It was the most useful I've felt this entire time."

"What did you two find when you were out there?" LeAnne asked, the edge in her voice unmistakable.

As always, Ned was the first one to address the unspoken questions hanging in the air. "Well, the only reason the rest of you got out of those woods alive was because we spent our time tracking down one ambush party after another and snuffing them out before they could hit you."

Rolling her eyes a bit, Sandra added, "We weren't quite the saviors of the group or anything, but we did our part."

"How many did you find?" Clint asked, making sure to ask Sandra directly.

"There were about two or three groups the first full day we were gone," she said. "That's why we didn't come back. They were swarming all over those woods and even around them to set up for an attack. Burt must have really wanted to hit you before you got out in the open or he wouldn't have spread his men so thin."

"Don't let her downplay it, Clint," Ned cut in. "We were one hell of a team. She could sniff them out a mile away so I could sneak in there and do all sorts of damage. I let their horses go, stole their guns. I even stole the boots away from some poor bastards when they were sleeping. You think you were cold? Try going through this shit without your boots!"

Everyone listening had a good laugh, which was desperately needed. Even Sandra broke down, letting out the loudest laugh of them all when Ned described the would-be ambushers trying to fight while hopping around in the snow and slipping on the ice.

But the laughter couldn't last forever and it was LeAnne who brought it to a halt when she asked, "So how many of them are left?"

Sandra's smile faded away and she shook her head.

"I killed a few," Ned said. "But only when I had to. The rest were thrown off the track or sent back with their tails between their legs. Besides, even if I killed all of them, would that be so bad? I mean, they are trying to kill us, unless you haven't noticed."

"I noticed," Clint said without emotion. "But that doesn't mean we have to be out for blood. Killing is always the last resort, no matter what."

"Yeah, well, things change out here, Adams. Out here, only the strong ones make it through and that includes knowing when to put someone in the ground."

"You're right," Clint agreed. "But I need know what we're dealing with. The more men of theirs that die, the more desperate the others get. We've got plenty to deal with out here between the weather and now our lack of supplies. The last thing we need is to stoke that gang's fire by giving them vengeance as a flag to rally around."

All this time, LeAnne had been watching and listening, not only to the others in her group but also to the other things going on. Having set O'Connover on the ground, she could move more easily and kept turning in place as though she was searching for something.

Before too long, she found it.

"It's not that much farther to the border," Sandra said. "And now that the storm's passed, we'll be able to make it a lot easier."

Mike glanced toward LeAnne and watched her ride to a spot about twenty yards away and drop down from her saddle. Turning back to face Clint and the others, he said, "Easier? Maybe you didn't notice that we're missing something here, like our goddamn wagon! And that wagon was filled with our supplies!"

LeAnne found what she'd been after and was now on her way back to the group, bringing it along with her.

"We can salvage some supplies," Clint said, not looking at what LeAnne was doing. "And I'm pretty sure there's a town not too far from here that won't take us too much out of our way."

"Yeah," Ned replied, "and that might be just where Burt's headed, and going there will drop us right back into—"

Ned was cut off when LeAnne rode up and dropped something in front of everyone there. It was a man. He was wounded but only enough to make walking difficult. He glared up at them wearing his fear just beneath the surface but close enough for everyone to see it.

"You want to know what's out there?" LeAnne asked. "You want to know what Burt's got planned? Why don't we just ask this guy?"

FORTY-TWO

Indeed, the storm had passed. At least the storm made of snow and ice had gone; another storm still threatened. Clint knew that whatever was left of Burt's gang was bearing down on them even though there wasn't a gunman in sight. If the stakes were half as high as O'Connover had mentioned, the gang would not stop until the whole matter was resolved one way or another.

As the group picked through the rubble of the cart to reclaim whatever supplies they could, Clint continued checking the horizon for more shapes and listening for the approach of horses. Judging by the speed with which everyone worked, he wasn't the only one feeling that storm lurking just around the corner.

In a matter of minutes, the group had taken what they could and ridden away. The gunman that LeAnne had found was bundled up in some of O'Connover's spare chains and taken along with them just like an item salvaged from the wreck. He was wrapped so tightly, in fact, that he looked like a giant worm struggling on the back of Ned's saddle. O'Connover rode with LeAnne, looking only slightly inconvenienced by comparison.

Sandra led them off the beaten trail they'd been following. Even she wasn't completely aware of where to find the town Clint had mentioned. He was certain of it, however, which was enough to get them all riding in that direction.

They rode in silence, concentrating on the trail before them as well as on their singular goal. Although the motives had shifted slightly, that one goal had remained the same. It was too late to change it now.

"There it is," Clint said, looking into the eastern horizon as the sun dipped down behind him.

They'd ridden all day and had made it within eyeshot of civilization just before nightfall.

"What's it called?" Mike asked.

"Wolf Valley." Clint paused for a second and rethought his answer. "At least that's what I think it was called."

LeAnne swung down from her saddle and stretched her legs. "I don't care what it's called, just so long as it's not far from the border." When she said that, she automatically shifted her eyes toward Sandra.

The scout was looking north as though she could see the promised land. "We're not far at all. I can almost smell Canada from here."

Ned's boots hit the snow with a solid crunch and he started working the kinks from his back. "You know what I can smell? Supper. And I'm surprised I can smell that much over the stench of this asshole strapped to my horse."

The man LeAnne had plucked from the ambush site said something, but his words were muffled by the bandanna that had been stuffed into his mouth earlier that day. Still, the angry tone of his voice was unmistakable.

Clint was the last one to swing down from his saddle. "Get him down from there, Ned. If we're going to have a good talk with our new friend, it'll have to be out here where we can have some privacy."

The steely edge in Clint's voice cut right to the gagged man's core.

Ned pulled the prisoner from the back of his saddle and dropped him unceremoniously onto the ground. He then yanked the bandanna from his mouth, which had become frozen to his lips by sweat and saliva. "I'll bet that our friend here is just dying to talk to us." Flipping his coat open to reveal the iron strapped around his waist, Ned added, "Isn't that right, friend?"

"Go f—"

The insult was cut short by a backhand from Ned, who then drew his pistol and jammed the barrel up under the man's chin. Until now, Clint had thought LeAnne was overly suspicious of Ned, simply because he hadn't proven to be anything but an asset. But seeing the crazed look that had suddenly come into Ned's eyes, Clint got an idea of what she'd been talking about.

Clint eyed Ned closely, preparing to jump the instant it looked as if Ned was going too far. The only reason he hadn't jumped in already was the expression on the captured man's face. He was as white as a ghost and his lip trembled as though he was about to cry. Instead of tears, however, words came spilling from his mouth.

FORTY-THREE

"This was the last attack, I swear to God," the prisoner sputtered. "If this one didn't do the trick, we all agreed to split up and meet up later."

"Meet where?" Clint asked.

"We didn't have time to plan. Burt's lost his mind and he was watching us all like a hawk. We barely had time to agree that this was the last order we meant to follow."

Pressing the gun up under the other man's chin a little more, Ned said, "That's bullshit. Burt's men don't abandon him like that. He makes it too profitable to stay. Besides that, there aren't many men that got the sand to walk out on Burt."

Clint turned his eyes toward Ned, suddenly seeing him in a whole new light. It didn't take razor-sharp instincts to know that Ned wasn't just talking about rumors he'd heard. Ned saw the look on Clint's face and shrugged.

"There aren't many men with that kind of sand," Ned explained. "But there's at least one that I know pretty well."

Putting his questions for Ned in the back of his mind, Clint turned once again to face the man squirming on the ground. Just looking at the captured man was enough to get him talking again.

"Burt's sick," the prisoner spat out. "He's burning up with fever and he's killed more of his men than you have."

"What?"

"He hears something he don't like, and he kills the man that said it. Something happens that he didn't plan, and he kills the man that did it. He's crazy, I tell you! He said that if we came back and O'Connover was still alive, none of us would be."

"And you believed him?" Clint said.

"Hell yes, we believed him. He talked tough plenty of times to keep us in line, but he only got rough to them that had it coming. The payoffs were worth the trouble, and this payoff was going to be the best yet."

"What kind of payoff?"

"Gold, cash, land, mines, even whole damn towns were up for grabs, and we would all split it up once we got rid of the men that own it all. Hell, Burt told us that we wouldn't have much trouble once we took out the one man at the top of that list."

"And who is that?" Clint asked, keeping his voice so level that nobody could know just how important the question was.

"Man by the name of Mays. Owen Mays. He heads up the group that took fortunes from folks up north of the border, and he's been real good at holding onto it. But Burt said he found a way to get to him and when we did, every penny Mays collected would be up for grabs."

"So why kill O'Connover?"

"Because he knows enough to put Mays and all them rich men out of business. Burt told us that all the rest of those men would sit tight until O'Connover came back because they wanted to ask who he talked to and what he said before they killed him themselves."

Everyone was gathered around the prisoner now. Even O'Connover was looking down at the man, not even mindful of his own chains.

"That's why they wanted me taken alive," O'Connover said.

The captive gang member nodded. Ned no longer had his pistol under the guy's chin. Enough had been said— he didn't need it there.

"Those rich men won't do a damn thing until they know they're safe and that O'Connover didn't say a word to a lawman that don't feed from their hands."

Mike stepped up and asked, "So this is all just a race to see who can take this Mays fella out first?"

The man on the ground thought about it for a second and shrugged. "Well, if you put it that way, yeah."

"How does Burt come by all this information?" Le-Anne asked.

But it wasn't the prisoner who answered. Ned did that for him. "It makes sense. Besides, Burt wouldn't leave anything to chance. Not with that much at stake. He had men looking in on Mays, didn't he?"

The man on the ground nodded vigorously. "He knew plenty of the men working for the fellows that Mays trusted. Plus, he got some of us in close enough to hear what we needed." Turning to Clint, he explained, "If O'Connover got into the wrong hands, Mays would either fall at the hands of the law or his partners. Either way, that didn't leave much for us."

"So you, Burt and the rest take O'Connover out of the picture yourselves and then swoop in to be the ones to take Mays down. But before you got to be the vultures on that corpse," Clint said, his words like salt in the other man's wounds, "the whole thing fell apart."

"Only because Burt lost his mind to the fever. We meant to wait it out once we saw he was sick, but he was taking out too many of us along the way and . . . well . . .

none of us were good enough to go against him directly. He don't sleep no more and he hardly even recognizes any of our faces. The best thing we could do was call it a loss and get as far away as we could before we wound up dead."

"Where were you supposed to meet?" Clint asked.

"I told you, we didn't have enough time to—"

Ned's pistol came up beneath the other man's chin so quickly that he didn't know it was there until he heard the hammer clicking back.

"That was the most important thing you men would have had to decide before splitting up," Clint said, jumping in while the panic was still fresh on the other man's face. "There's no way in hell you'd leave without arranging some meeting place, even if it was just to check in before moving on."

"I told you! We didn't get a chance!"

Looking into the other man's eyes, Ned smiled like a snake that was just about to devour a crippled mouse. "Then you're pretty much less than worthless, ain't ya?"

Clint didn't much approve of Ned's way of going about things, but it was late, and he was cold and tired. Besides, all he needed to do was keep quiet long enough for the other man to start worrying again.

"Emmerow!" The other man shouted. "It's about half a day's ride northwest of the Montana border. I swear to God, we're meeting in Emmerow."

Clint looked over to Sandra and got a confirming nod.

"I've heard of it," she said.

He may not have agreed with Ned's methods, but Clint couldn't argue with the results. He'd become an expert at reading men's faces and Clint had no doubt that the man on the ground was telling the truth.

"All right then," Clint said. "Looks like we've got just a bit more work to do."

FORTY-FOUR

Three horses rode into Wolf Valley that night. All three of the riders were bundled in layers of clothing to protect them from the harshness of the winter night, though the chill felt warm compared to what they'd gotten used to. Only one of them, however, wore chains beneath his clothing to keep his hands bound together and his entire body tied to the back of his horse.

O'Connover wasn't struggling to get out of his chains any longer, though. In fact, he was a willing participant in what Clint had planned for him. Clint rode at the front of the trio with O'Connover and LeAnne not too far behind. Any other time, the sight of the town would have been like a vision from heaven. They weren't yet in the mood to celebrate, however.

"This won't take long," Clint said as he came to a stop. Swinging down from Eclipse's back, he tied the horse up to a small shack next to a general store. "Keep an eye on him and keep riding like we discussed. If you run into trouble—"

"I can handle myself, Clint. You know that," LeAnne said.

Nodding, Clint replied, "I know. But now's not the

180

time to take chances. The whole reason we brought him along with us was so we could keep an eye on him."

"Mike could've done it."

"He's busy looking over the new friend you found for us."

LeAnne let out a deep breath and nodded. "You're right. I just wish this was over. I want to finish this so I can sleep in a real bed, have some real food and warm my hands by a fire bigger than a spark."

"Don't mention food," Clint grumbled. "I want all of that as much as you, but if we don't do this right, things will just end up twice as bad as they were when they started. We've got a real chance here and I doubt it'll come again."

"Burt could just die, you know. If he's got such a bad fever, he could be dead already."

"Yeah, but don't count on it. Men like him are too tough to die from a fever. Our biggest mistake would be to assume otherwise. Now just keep going and I'll meet up with you in a bit."

Clint and the other two parted ways. LeAnne rode off, leading O'Connover's horse by its reins while Clint headed into the small building. He was only in there for a couple minutes, but it felt like hours before he walked out again.

The remnants of clouds overhead had swallowed up the sun. A partial moon was enough to give the ground its all-too-familiar pale glow. Clint stepped out of the building and walked over to pat Eclipse on the nose. From there, he headed toward the sound of voices and music coming from a nearby saloon.

"You son of a bitch," came a haggard, wheezing voice.

Clint started to turn but made it only halfway before he saw a flicker of movement out of the corner of his eye.

"I got the drop on you, bastard. I always knew I'd wind up having to do this myself."

"I guess that would make you Burt," Clint said, slowly turning just his head to get a look at the other man.

"You'd guess right, Adams." Burt stood across the street, holding a pistol at hip level. His hand wasn't completely steady, but it was steady enough to keep the weapon aimed squarely at Clint's chest. "I'll bet you don't even remember me."

Clint took the opportunity to study Burt carefully. "Can't say as I ever met you, but I've sure been hearing a lot about you lately."

"Yeah. I'll just bet you have." Burt's eyes darted for a second but not far from his target. He seemed to be looking at something flying through the air that only he could see.

"You're sick, Burt."

"What're you now? A doctor?"

"No, but it would take a blind man to miss the fact that you're not right." As he spoke, Clint looked over the other man and saw a dozen things that weren't right. Burt's coat was unbuttoned, his steps were unsteady, even his breathing was so rough that it shook his entire body. "Put the gun down and we can get you to a doctor."

"You'd like that, I'd wager. I bet that's how you got your reputation, Adams. Talk a man into trusting you and then shoot him in the back. The rest of the world calls you the big, bad Gunsmith."

All this time, Clint had been moving himself slowly into position. By now, he was facing Burt and had even put himself a comfortable distance from the fevered man. His hand was inching toward the Colt at his side, but Clint could tell he wouldn't be able to get much farther. Burt's fuse was almost burnt out.

"Hand over O'Connover," Burt demanded.

"I don't have him with me."

"Then what were you doing in that little house?"

"That's a telegraph office. I contacted some Canadian

lawmen that I can trust. O'Connover's going to be handed over to them and then this whole thing'll be over."

Burt's eyes widened and he fought to keep his focus on Clint. "What? Why'd you do that? We could have been rich, Adams. You and me." He clenched his eyes shut and shook his head. "I mean I could be rich. Me and the men that stuck with me. There's others, you know. Not all of 'em were swallowed up by the devil in the storm."

"The devil in the storm?"

"I seen him, Adams. He had a white face with long teeth and eyes like a cat. They were yellow eyes, Adams. I seen 'em myself."

Burt had talked long enough for Clint to ease his hand close enough to his Colt for all of his worries to fade away. Now that he'd set himself up with the winning cards, all he had to do was play them.

"Burt, listen to me. You need to get some rest or this fever will kill you. You're seeing things. If you wait too much longer a doctor won't be able to do anything for you."

"I been trying to kill you all this time, Adams. Why should I stop now?"

It was a reasonable question. And the sad fact was that no matter what answer he gave, Clint knew Burt would charge right ahead, fever or not. Men like him always did.

"I've spoken to the Lord God Almighty!" Burt wheezed. "He said that storm was sent to teach us that only the strong survive. Remember that, Adams! Only the strong."

Clint's mind was clear as day and every muscle in his body had been waiting for the signal that Burt had passed the point of no return. When he saw that Burt was able to take a shot, he let his reflexes flow.

Clint's arm snapped down and he drew the Colt in a move so fluid that none of the cowering bystanders would ever recall seeing him clear leather. They saw only the flash of sparks from Clint's modified pistol and heard only the shot that put Burt down like a wounded animal.

But Clint wasn't about to rest just yet. For some reason, he believed a few things Burt had said. And if one of them was correct, there were still a few loose cannons out there gunning for their prize.

FORTY-FIVE

Clint turned the corner and saw LeAnne and O'Connover waiting at the end of the street. Burt's words flew through his mind and when he spotted two figures stepping out from the shadows with guns drawn, he knew he'd taken too much time dealing with the fevered gang leader.

From Clint's angle, he could see the two gunmen. LeAnne and O'Connover, however, weren't so lucky. Clint lifted his Colt and started figuring out his shot, unsure if he could drop both of the gunmen before they managed to fire.

Before Clint could squeeze his trigger, a rifle shot cracked through the air from above and behind him. It came from the roof of the saloon on the corner and blasted one of the shadowy figures off his feet.

Clint looked up and saw Ned waving down at him. Clint briefly wondered why Ned wasn't taking aim at the second gunman, but when he looked back at the final gang member, Clint saw the outlaw already lowering his pistol.

Another shadowy figure had crept up behind the gunman and wrapped one arm around his neck. The other hand held a familiar knife against the gunman's throat. It was Sandra.

"What do you say, Adams?" she asked as she turned the gunman away from a gaping O'Connover. "Is there room for one more on the last leg of our trip?"

Having weathered one hell of a storm, the party found the rest of the ride into Canada just plain easy. The lawmen Clint had contacted were only too eager to arrange to take the prisoners off their hands. The two captured gang members were too tired to put up much of a fight, and O'Connover looked positively relieved.

"I guess things turned out for the best," O'Connover said. "Even though I'll still probably wind up with a noose around my neck."

"I doubt that," Clint replied. "You'll answer for your crimes, but you'll also be the man who speaks out against Owen Mays. That'll buy you some leeway. Besides, I'm coming along to see you safely into good hands. Wainwright is a good lawman and he'll see to it you get a fair trial. I doubt we'll have much to worry about when it comes to any more hired guns. We've already seen how quickly rats like them flee a sinking ship."

One of the Canadians, a young lawman with a square jaw and tanned, leathery skin, nodded and said, "Wainwright sends his best and told me to tell you he'll meet us when he gets back from Emmerow. Apparently, he has some business to wrap up there. The trial will take place as soon as possible. We've been looking for whoever's behind these incidents you described for some time."

Clint turned to where Ned, Sandra and Mike were standing. "I guess this is it. There's no need for you to go any farther, especially since you helped us all so much already."

Ned moved closer to Clint. Because they were short one horse, he carried Sandra on the back of his saddle. Extending a hand, Ned said, "It was damn fine to meet you, Clint."

"Same here, Ned. I'd ride with you anytime."

Grinning, Ned answered, "I just may take you up on that."

Sandra was next and she leaned over to give him a quick kiss on the cheek before whispering, "Good-bye. And thanks."

"No, thank you," Clint said.

The Canadian lawman handed Clint a heavy pouch, which Clint dipped his hand into and then handed over to Sandra. "That's the reward being offered for these men. Since we rounded up the entire gang, there's actually a bit more in there than Bobby figured. And LeAnne," Clint said, turning to her while holding out the money he'd taken from the pouch before handing it over, "here's the share for you and Bobby. That should be plenty to—"

"Keep it," she interrupted.

"Keep it? Why?"

"Well, at least keep it for the time being," she added. "I'm coming with you to see this through. Call me suspicious, but I want to see it to the end. Besides, I've never really been to a trial before."

"I'm heading off with them," Mike said, nodding toward Ned and Sandra. "I've had my fill of this whole damn thing." He shook Clint's hand and rode away without another word.

The lawmen took their prisoners into custody. From there, the party split in two. One group headed south back into the States while Clint, LeAnne, the law and their prisoners all continued north.

"I've been meaning to ask you something, Clint," LeAnne said.

"Go ahead and ask."

"What did Bobby Hill ever do for you that counted for so much?"

Clint smirked and replied, "Let's just say it's part of the reason why I can't stomach the taste of whiskey to this very day."

Watch for

ROLLING THUNDER

277th novel in the exciting GUNSMITH
series from Jove

Coming in January!